#16 EERIE IN THE MIRROR

#16 EERIE IN THE MIRROR

ROBERT JAMES

Based upon the television series "Eerie Indiana" created by Karl Schaefer and José Rivera

AN AVON  CAMELOT BOOK

AVON BOOKS, INC.
1350 Avenue of the Americas
New York, New York 10019

First Avon Camelot Printing: November 1998

CAMELOT TRADEMARK REG. U.S. PAT. OFF. AND IN OTHER COUNTRIES, MARCA REGISTRADA, HECHO EN U.S.A.

Printed in the U.S.A.

OPM   10 9 8 7 6 5 4 3 2 1

PROLOGUE

PROLOGUE

*M*y name is Mitchell Taylor. Not too long ago, I lived an ordinary, peaceful existence in the most normal city in the entire world—Eerie, Indiana. Life here was so boring people read the phone book for excitement.

Then a new cable TV guy moved in and weird things started happening. One of his channels linked us to another Eerie, stranger and more bizarre than anything you can imagine. Before the link was shut down, all sorts of weird things had oozed across from the other Eerie to ours, and had settled down to stay.

Sure, the place still *looks* normal—mostly. But if you examine things closely, you'll find there's a lot more to Eerie than meets the eye.

Item: The law of gravity is suspended on alternate Thursday nights from nine to twelve.

Item: The Loch Ness monster lives in the sewer system.

Item: The local hot-dog vendor is a witch.

Every time something bizarre happens, I think life just can't get any weirder. Then I turn the corner and find something even stranger waiting to shake my hand. But no matter how weird Eerie gets, nobody seems to notice.

Nobody except my friend Stanley. Stanley is my next-door neighbor, and the only person I can count on when things get truly freaky. Together, we're keeping a record of all the stuff that happens around here. We hope someday to use it to return the city to its rightful state—boring.

Don't believe me? You will.

1

*M*irrors distort things. I'm not just talking about funhouse mirrors, which make you look fat, or taller than Shaquille O'Neal. I'm talking about *all* mirrors.

I'm sure you've seen those warnings on car mirrors about things being closer than they may appear. In my opinion, mirrors ought to carry another warning—what you're looking at is the opposite of reality.

And the last thing you want to do is have opposites touch each other.

Or let me put it another way: if the *real you* ever meets the *mirror* you, there'll be plenty of trouble.

It happened the same day I brushed my teeth with shampoo. Not that I set out to learn a lesson about mirrors. Or to brush my teeth with hair soap.

It was a Saturday morning. I had stayed up late the

night before, watching a National Geographic special called *In Search of the Wild Anteater*. It was a pretty cool show, especially if you don't like ants. The point is, I got out of bed still sleepy. When I went to the bathroom to wash up, I found that the lightbulb had burned out. The entire room was dark and shadowy. I could barely see my face in the mirror. I stared for a few seconds, trying to see the image clearly. Maybe my eyes weren't focused, or maybe the dimness threw everything off. But whatever the reason, all I could see was a blurry fog where my face should be.

I kept looking at the mirror as I groped for my toothbrush. Ordinarily, I like to start out the day by clearing the night gook out of my mouth. Nothing's worse than putting a spoonful of sugar-coated cornflakes in your mouth and tasting night gook instead.

The gook was especially thick this particular morning. I've always wondered exactly how it gets there. Is there a gook fairy who comes around at night, kind of like the tooth fairy in reverse?

Anyway, this morning my quest for good oral hygiene backfired. As I stared at the mirror I grabbed a tube that felt like the toothpaste. I squirted it on the brush and opened wide.

I spit so hard I nearly sent my tongue down the drain.

I guess it could have been worse. I could have been in the shower and used toothpaste to wash my hair. And looking on the bright side, my gums won't be getting dandruff any time soon.

I was still tasting shampoo when I went down to the kitchen. The rest of my family was already there, having breakfast. Mom was cooking and working on a new computer program at the same time. She set up her laptop on the counter next to the stove. She flipped eggs with one hand and typed with the other. Dad and my sister, Kari, were reading different parts of the newspaper.

"Light's out in the bathroom," I told my father.

Dad gave me a puzzled expression. "Is that a new rock group?"

"No. The lightbulb burned out in the bathroom. I brushed my teeth with shampoo."

"I wouldn't use shampoo on your teeth," said my dad. "There's no fluoride in it."

"Listen to this. The producers of *As Eerie Turns* are looking for extras," announced Kari. "There's a casting call today at the town hall. Mom, can I try out? I'd just love to be on a soap opera."

"Eat your eggs first, dear," said my mom.

"Dad, the lightbulb has to be replaced in the bathroom," I said. "There's no light in there."

"That's not scientifically correct," said my father. He's a scientist, and he's always saying stuff like that. "Light exists everywhere. That is because it is actually energy, the by-product of displacement at the atomic level. The question is whether we can see it or not.''

"The by-product over the mirror is burned out," I said.

"It will have to be replaced then," he said. "Otherwise we won't be able to see what we're doing. We may brush our teeth with shampoo."

"That's what I was trying to tell you."

"The physics of the lightbulb are very interesting," continued my father. "The lightbulb can serve as a model for the way the universe works. . . ."

When you're a scientist, I guess nearly everything can serve as a model for the way the universe works. Just last week, Dad had used a stick of butter and a bowl of overcooked peas to explain the difference between energy and matter.

I couldn't follow his explanation, but I did get out of eating my peas.

The doorbell saved me from a long lecture on lightbulbs and the universe. "I'll get it," I yelled, jumping up from the table.

When I opened the front door, I found Stanley on the front stoop. He had his backpack with him.

"Hey, Mitchell. Are you ready or what?" he asked.

"I was just having some breakfast."

"Thought you'd never ask," he said, barging inside as though I had invited him.

6

Mom didn't seem to mind. She put another Pop-Tart in the toaster and fixed him some eggs. Dad had gone off to replace the bathroom light. Kari was already on the phone with one of her friends, telling her about the casting call for the soap opera.

"What are you boys up to today?" Mom asked as the eggs cooked.

"We're going to examine the borders of weirdness," Stanley said cheerfully.

"You're not still on that weirdness thing, are you?" my mom asked, shaking her head. "Honestly, guys, I would think you'd have better things to do with your time."

"It's serious, Mom," I told her for the thousandth time. "Weird things are happening all around us. Just the other day, I saw a tail sticking up in the kitchen sink."

"The Loch Ness monster, I suppose," said my mother.

"You saw him, too?" Stanley asked.

"Stanley. Mitchell." Mom shook her head as if we had just tried to convince her that the world was flat. "The next thing you're going to say is that Bigfoot is eating out of the garbage."

"It was the abominable snowman!" I said.

My mom just rolled her eyes. No matter how many times I tried explaining about how the weirdness had leaked into Eerie across a cable television channel, not even my own parents believed me.

Not that I blamed them. I wouldn't believe me either if I hadn't been there when it happened. That's why Stanley and I had decided to collect enough evidence to provide definite proof. We had sworn a sacred vow to work night and day without rest until we succeeded.

Unless there was something good on TV, of course.

This morning we had a new project lined up. We were going to measure exactly how far the weirdness extended in the town. We wanted to know the borders of strange.

"Maybe you should go downtown with your sister and see about auditioning for the soap opera," Mom suggested to me. "You'd like to be a star, wouldn't you?"

"Not really," I said.

"I think you should go."

"Mother, I r-e-a-l-l-l-y don't think I should have to have a little brother tagging along on my big day," protested Kari as she hung up the phone. Her words had a funny accent. I guess she thought she sounded like a Hollywood star.

To me, it sounded like she had a grapefruit up her nose.

"Believe me, I don't want to tag along," I told her.

"Thank goodness," she said, fluttering her eyelashes.

"Do you have something in your eye, Kari?" asked Stanley.

"No, dear," she answered. "This is just something we stars do."

Stanley and I exchanged glances. Hollywood had already gone to Kari's head.

"Are you sure you don't want to go?" my mother asked me.

"Definitely," I replied.

"Suit yourself," said my mom. "Stanley, would you like your Pop-Tart buttered?"

After breakfast, Stanley and I mapped out our strategy. Stanley had borrowed a collection of rulers and other measuring instruments from his father. They were already loaded into his backpack. He'd also brought along some supplies that generally come in useful when you're dealing with strangeness:

1. magnifying glass, for a closeup inspection
2. notebook, to record observations
3. frozen pizza, in case we got hungry and there happened to be a microwave handy
4. *Pro-Football Digest* (If things got boring, Stanley planned to read it. He wants to be the first kid in town to correctly predict who will win next year's Super Bowl.)

5. the *Farmer's Almanac* (Just because.)
6. clean underwear (You never know what you'll run into.)

My contribution to our expedition consisted of a homemade weirdness detector. The major part was a portable television. Technically, the TV belonged to Kari. But since she was going to spend the entire day at the audition, she wouldn't be needing it. She would gladly lend it to us, especially for something this important.

Not.

But since she was going to be gone all day, she'd never know it was missing. What she didn't know wouldn't hurt her—or me, in this instance. The television had a 9-inch screen and worked off a battery. The picture was black-and-white. Kari used it mostly to watch talk show reruns, but that didn't seem to have harmed it.

Ever since the weirdness hit Eerie, a strange phenomenon had affected all of the TV sets in town. Whether they were connected to cable or not, they all received the two thousand channels provided by the Eerie Cable Company. I had first noticed this phenomenon a few days before, in Mr. Crawford's store. Every set in his TV section worked perfectly, even though they weren't hooked up. A lot of weird things have been happening there, so I didn't make too much of it. Then I came home and saw the cable on our TV was unplugged—but our reception was perfect. The same thing happened at Stanley's house.

That gave me an idea. I figured that all we had to do was carry a TV set around, watching it until the reception fuzzed out. That would show us how far the weirdness went.

Stanley and I wired some other things to the TV, hoping to show which direction the weirdness came from. There was my mom's radar detector, a fish finder my father had bought at a garage sale but never used, and an old electric razor.

The razor didn't really help the detection, but I thought it might be handy. Finding the edge of strange might be a hair-raising experience.

"Working perfectly," said Stanley when we tested it in my backyard. He flipped through the television channels. "Hey, did you know there's a twenty-four-hour Mr. Magoo Network? Wow."

"You can check it out later," I told him. "We have weirdness to detect."

"I just love it when he runs his car into the wall."

"He does that every cartoon."

"I know, and I love it," said Stanley, trotting to keep up. Honestly, sometimes I think Eerie has gotten to him.

We headed east first. Dad always says strange things

happen "back east," so it seemed logical to go that way.

The TV got a clear picture all the way up to Mockingbird Lane, out past the cemetery. I kind of expected it would, since the city line was still about a quarter of a mile away. What I hadn't counted on was taking so long to reach the border. Stanley kept getting interested in different programs. It took us more than an hour just to get past the cemetery.

"Look, Mitch—*Bonnie and Clyde,*" he said, flipping the channels. "Wow, look at this gunfight. Cool."

"We can't spend all morning watching television," I told him. I switched off the set and began walking toward Mirror Boulevard.

It's more a country road than a boulevard. I don't know why they called it a boulevard, but I do know where *Mirror* came from. There used to be a mirror factory on the block. It closed down years ago. High fences, a burned-out building and millions of shards of broken glass are the only things left. By my calculation, whoever owned the factory has about five centuries of bad luck coming to him.

"You don't understand," Stanley protested as we walked. "That was *Bonnie and Clyde.* One of the best gangster movies ever made."

"One of the goriest, you mean." I continued walking. The edge of town lay only twenty yards away.

"What a spoilsport," Stanley groused as he caught up. "Can't you stand a fun movie every so often?"

"What's fun about a movie where people rob banks?" I asked.

"Robbing banks is cool, Mitchell."

"Really? Would you like it if somebody robbed our bank, the Eerie Trust a Lot and Save a Little?"

Stanley had a savings account there: $4.38.

"Sure, if it was a movie," he said.

"Great. I'll put a note on the door that says anyone who wants to rob your savings account is welcome to it. As long as they make a movie out of it." I stopped and turned on the TV, making sure not to turn to the channel showing *Bonnie and Clyde.*

A rerun of *Romper Room* filled the screen. Channel 372—all *Romper Room,* all the time.

Meanwhile, Stanley was getting very bored. As I paused to check the TV, he picked up a rock from the side of the road. I stopped him before he could throw it at the factory ruins.

"Don't do that, Stanley. If you happen to break a piece of a mirror, it will bring bad luck."

"You really are getting to be a pain, Mitch," he said, twisting out of my grip. "Besides, there's nothing left in there to break."

He flung the rock in a high arc over the fence toward the building. A fire had wiped out the roof years ago.

Stanley's rock sailed over the nearest wall, into the depths of the factory.

Where there was at least one mirror left.

Until Stanley's rock hit it, that is. The crash echoed across the street.

I shook my head. "There you go. Bad luck."

"Aw, Mitch, you don't believe in that, do you?" said Stanley, stooping down to grab another rock.

Just then, the TV screen went blank, and the loud hissing of static filled our ears.

2

We crouched over the television set, flipping the channels back and forth. The only thing we could pick up was static and more static.

"This must be it," said Stanley. "The edge of weirdness."

"Could be," I said, trying to stay calm. I switched on the rest of the equipment. Except for a school of goldfish in the nearby sewer, the fish finder's screen was clear. But the razor sounded a little off-key.

"Let's write down the location in the notebook," I said. "And then see if we can find the other side."

Stanley took a long folding ruler from his knapsack. It was an old-fashioned measuring stick used by carpenters.

"Measure from here to the lamppost," I advised him. "That will give us something solid as a point of reference."

The lamppost was beyond the ruler's reach. In fact,

Stanley had to use two other rulers to find the distance. One was the retracting steel type that builders use. The other was his mom's sewing tape. We laid them down carefully, end to end.

"Thirty-two feet, seven inches. Give or take a thumbnail," he announced.

"Why a thumbnail?"

"I had to hold the ruler down with something." Stanley packed the rulers away in his backpack. "Looks like we were right about the city line being the border," he added, pointing across the street at a sign that read CITY LIMITS.

"Let's not jump to conclusions. The TV was working fine until you threw the stone."

"You don't think that rock had anything to do with it, do you?" Stanley asked.

"No. But I can't explain why the TV was working one second and then wasn't working the next."

"You must have moved it when you heard the rock hit the mirror."

"The TV was right here on the ground," I said. "I was ten feet away."

"Let's not worry about it," said Stanley, fiddling with the equipment. The static got louder. The sound coming from the TV speaker was a little like a blender running in reverse. "All that's important is that we found the boundary."

"I'd still like to have an explanation on why it suddenly changed."

"Why do you need to explain everything?" Stanley asked. "If you saw a train coming down the street, would you look for the tracks? Or would you jump out of the way?"

"Both," I said.

He shook his head. "Some things you just have to accept. We are in Eerie, after all."

Stanley was right. Still, if my theory was correct, the television should start working again on the other side of the border. I picked it up and walked a few feet down Mirror Boulevard, back toward town. Sure enough, the television reception came right back.

Sort of.

I put the TV down and stared at the screen.

"Now what?" Stanley asked.

"I just realized something. This is *Gilligan's Island.*"

"Oh yeah. I've seen that one. They find this box on the beach and—"

"But I had it on three seventy-two, the all *Romper Room,* all the time channel. Remember?"

Stanley hit the display button. The number 372 popped up on the screen.

"That's weird," I told him. "I know this is supposed to be the *Romper Room* station. What channel was *Bonnie and Clyde* on?"

"MMN—the Mayhem and Madness Network," said Stanley. "Channel fifteen."

I flipped the selector to 15. But instead of MMN, the Romance Network logo filled the screen.

"Maybe they're changing the channel lineup," suggested Stanley. "They do it all the time."

That didn't make a lot of sense to me. But I decided not to say anything. Stanley was right. You couldn't expect everything that happened in Eerie to have an explanation.

After all, that was the point about being the center of strange for the entire planet.

We picked up the TV and headed off toward the other side of town, looking for the other end of strange. Every so often we stopped and turned the TV back on, checking the reception. It was still sharp, but the channels remained mixed up.

When we reached the center of town, we saw that at least half the citizens of Eerie had come to audition for the soap opera. A line of people snaked out the door of the town hall, down Main Street, and around the giant statue of an ear of corn in the town square. I hadn't seen so many people here since Tommy Peterson claimed he found a gold nugget in the street near O'Brien's Real Italian Delicatessen. Half of Eerie was dug up by prospectors before Lisa Leterri realized it was a gold filling she'd lost chewing a cannoli from the deli.

"Say, Mitchell, can statues move?" Stanley asked, staring at the crowd.

"Not ordinarily."

"The front of that ear of corn used to face the town hall, didn't it?"

Stanley was right. The giant ear of corn now had its back to the city building.

"Think someone moved it?" he asked.

"It looks kind of heavy for someone to move."

"Maybe it moved on its own," suggested Stanley.

"If it did, then that's pretty weird. It would also be the proof we need to show people that weird things are happening," I said. "Everyone knows statues don't move."

"Maybe it's a political statement," said Stanley. "Since it turned its back on the town hall. Or do you think it just wanted a better view of World of Stuff?"

A good question. In either case, this needed to be investigated.

"We should make this our top priority," I told my buddy. "We can map the other border of weirdness later. Let's check and see if there are signs of the statue being moved."

"Right now? I'm hungry. Let's eat the pizza."

"It's probably still frozen," I warned him as he un-zipped his backpack.

"It's melted a little around the edges," he said, inspecting the package. He broke open the plastic and took a nibble. "Mmm—kind of like pizza ice cream."

"I really think we ought to find a microwave to cook it in."

Stanley nearly chipped a tooth trying to take a bite. "All right," he said, rubbing his mouth. "Think Mr. Crawford will let us use his microwave?"

Ordinarily, he probably would. But people were jammed six-deep on the sidewalk in front of the store, waiting to get in.

"He looks too busy," I told Stanley.

"Wow. Think he has another half-price sale on hula hoops?"

"Must be the crowd from the soap opera," I said. "Come on, let's go back to my house and use our microwave. We ought to make a plan for the statue investigation anyway."

Excited that we were really on to something at last, we used our best shortcuts to get home. Hopping over Mr. Wilson's fence, I slipped and fell right into his carp pond. Stanley laughed so hard his face almost slipped off his head.

"Somebody must have moved this pond," I groused.

"Oh, come on, Mitch. Get real. Nobody moves a pond."

"My sister's going to kill me," I said, holding up the television. It was covered with muck and pond scum.

Stanley dried the controls with his sweatshirt. Then he flipped it on. When nothing appeared on the screen, he gave it a good shake.

A small Japanese carp squirted out of the speaker panel and flipped right into the pond. Then the picture snapped on. It was the Eerie Home Shopping Network, selling miniature goldfish bowls.

"Good as new," said Stanley. "Except for the mud and slime."

I took the TV and tried cleaning it as we continued on our way. A few yards later, it was my turn to laugh. Stanley tripped over a garden hose and fell through the laundry Mrs. Smith had hung out to dry. A towel got wrapped around his head and he felt *splat* into a kiddie pool.

"This baby pool wasn't here yesterday!" he squealed. He dried himself off as best he could with the towel, then replaced it on the line.

"Good as new, except for the dirt," he said. "Think Mrs. Smith will notice?"

I shrugged. It was hard to say what anyone noticed in Eerie these days.

Stanley's sneakers were so wet they squished. We both felt like we had just run through a car wash. His backpack looked like it belonged to a fish.

And what was inside was no longer a frozen pizza. It was more like pizza soup.

"Doesn't taste that bad," he said, taking a lick off his finger.

Just the idea made my stomach turn. "Go get changed," I told him. "I'll go back to my house and have another pizza ready when you get there."

"What's wrong with this one?" Stanley asked.

"I don't like to use a spoon when I eat pizza."

"What if we put it in a toaster and dry it out?"

"Just get changed," I told him, starting away. "I'll find something else for us to eat. We have a lot to do this afternoon."

Even though I was sopping wet, I was still pretty excited. I trotted home, planning our next move. I figured the statue was the key to proving that weird things were going on in town. I kept running until I reached my front stoop. As I paused to retrieve my key from my pocket, the door flew open.

"Mitchell! Quick—get inside before the police find you!"

Stanley was standing in the middle of my doorway.

3

"*H*ow'd you get here so fast?" I demanded.

"What do you mean? I've been here all day."

"No, you haven't."

Before I could say anything else, Stanley grabbed my shirt and pulled me inside. "You're lucky the police haven't found you. They've been cruising up and down the block all morning. I barely had a chance to finish eating my lunch. Too bad you missed it," he added. "It was pepperoni chili. Your favorite."

"What police?"

"The ones who are trying to get the reward for capturing us," said Stanley. "What's with you, anyway? How come your clothes are all wet? And where'd you get the TV?"

Words sputtered from my mouth. I was so exasperated I couldn't even speak coherently. Stanley was acting as if he hadn't been with me all morning. Even weirder, he was pretending this was his house. I glanced around the room. It absolutely was my house. Mom's couch with its yellow-green plaid upholstery sat across from me. My dad's EZ-Boy recliner, with deluxe cup holder and built-in fly swatter, sat right next to it.

"Go upstairs and change," Stanley said, pushing me toward the stairs. "Put on your spare set of jeans from my dresser."

I couldn't tell whether this was some sort of joke he was playing or what. I did have a spare set of clothes at Stanley's house—but that was next door.

He seemed to believe that he was really in his own house. One other thing seemed odd. Stanley was wearing different clothes from the ones he'd been wearing when he fell into the kiddie pool. I had trouble believing that he had changed so quickly and still beaten me here.

And what was all this about the police?

My own clothes were still soaking wet, so I decided to go ahead and get changed. Maybe by the time I came back down Stanley would be off this kick and have an explanation.

"Wait a second," he said as I started for the stairs. I turned around, expecting to see him break into a smile. Instead, he grabbed the portable TV and the rest of the equipment from me.

"We ought to get ten bucks for this TV set at the

pawn shop," he said. "But this other stuff's just worthless junk."

"That's my sister's TV," I said.

"Your sister? She's out of jail?"

"My sister has never been in jail."

Stanley gave me a strange look. "Did you bump your head?"

"Bump my head? What are you talking about?"

"It's OK, buddy," he said, patting my shoulder. "We'll get out of this. I promise."

Confused, I left him downstairs and went to get changed. One thing I'll say about Stanley, he can carry a joke pretty far. Even so, I couldn't understand why he was kidding around. Now that we had spotted the change in the statue, there was a lot of work to be done. We were on the edge of a very important weirdness breakthrough.

Then I walked into the room that should have been my bedroom. It looked exactly like Stanley's room.

Weirdness had come up and smacked me right between the eyes.

4

At first I wasn't sure what to do. Then I realized that being confused and dry was better than being confused and wet. I went to Stanley's dresser and pulled open the bottom drawer. Sure enough, my spare jeans were there, along with a Green Bay Packers T-shirt. I had left them both at Stanley's house six months before.

A photograph stood on the top of the dresser. Stanley sat in the middle of the picture, flanked by his parents.

My mom and dad.

I went to the mirror in the bathroom, just to make sure I was still me.

I looked almost like me. Almost, but not quite.

My spare set of clothes didn't fit quite right. The button on the jeans wouldn't snap shut, and the hole for my head in the T-shirt was too tight.

I decided to blow-dry myself with the hair dryer. It

took fifteen minutes. I was dry, but as mixed up as ever. Over and over I asked myself two questions:

Had Stanley gone crazy, or had I?

Had we somehow switched places?

The one person in Eerie I could always count on was Stanley. We had been friends for years. Up until now, we had always investigated weirdness together. Now he seemed to be part of it.

Or was I the strange one? Could I have imagined my entire life up until now? Was my past a hallucination?

I shuddered at the idea.

"Mitch! Mitch! Quick! Get down here!" Stanley shouted.

I bolted from the room and ran down to my friend. I found him crouched in front of the living-room window.

"Stanley, there's something we have to talk about."

He shushed me, then pointed toward the window. I looked out and saw a police car in the roadway.

I noticed right away that the car wasn't a regular police car. It had a bar of lights and the words *Eerie Police* on the side, all right. But it was very old. Oh, it shined as if it had recently been polished. But the model seemed to have come from the 1920s. In fact, it looked like one of the cool old cars in the *Bonnie & Clyde* movie.

"He just pulled up," Stanley told me. "Did he follow you here?"

"No, but . . . listen, we have to talk."

Before Stanley could answer, we heard the wail of a siren from down the block. Two more police cars skidded to a stop. They looked exactly like the first. Then a large black truck rumbled in behind them. It also looked like an old model.

"SWAT team!" cried Stanley. "Out the back, quick!"

He pushed me toward the back door before I could say anything. When we reached the kitchen, he grabbed me by the arm and pulled me down.

"Stanley, what's going on?" I asked.

"The police are trying to surround the place, buddy," he said. He ran to a cupboard where my mom—or his mom—kept plates.

At least, she used to. When he opened it up he pulled out two violin cases.

"When did you start playing the violin?" I asked.

"Very funny," he said, snapping open one of the cases.

Inside was a tommy gun—the same kind of submachine gun as the ones used by Bonnie and Clyde. He tossed it to me. Then he opened up the other case and took one for himself.

The gun was heavy and smelled of oil and gunpowder. I had held guns before—I took a rifle safety course when I was in the Eerie Scouts—but this was more than a little scary. It was very, very dangerous.

"All right, Mitchell Taylor! We know you're in there! Come out with your hands up!" yelled a police officer over a bullhorn.

"You'll never take us alive, copper!" Stanley screamed back.

"I wouldn't go quite *that* far," I told Stanley.

"Relax, Mitch. All we have to do is make it to the secret passageway in the back. Then we can sneak out and go ahead with our plan to rob the Eerie Trust a Lot and Save a Little this afternoon."

"We're robbing the bank this afternoon?"

"As long as we get there by five. Otherwise we'll have to wait until Monday." Stanley shook his head. "I don't see why banks can't be open seven days a week. I mean, if they're going to open on Saturday, why not Sunday, too?"

"Why are we robbing the bank?"

Stanley gave me an odd look. "That must have been some knock you took on the head, huh?"

"No, you don't understand. A few minutes ago, you and I were cutting through Mr. Wilson's backyard—"

"And we ran into Dennis the Menace, right?"

"No."

"Duh. I was being sarcastic, Mitch. You and I haven't seen each other since we knocked over that bank down in Normal three days ago. Say, you're not trying to get out of giving me my share of the loot, are you?"

"No."

He eyed me suspiciously. Before I could say anything else, something crashed through the front window.

"Tear gas!" he yelled, jumping up. He opened the back door. "Let's do it!"

Stanley rolled outside as another canister of tear gas broke through the window. Already my eyes were starting to sting as the fumes spread out. I dropped to the floor and crawled as quickly as I could to the doorway. I decided to leave the tommy gun inside—it was too dangerous to take with me. And I sure wasn't going to use it to rob a bank.

I could hear a commotion in front of the house. Holding my breath, I dove out, rolling onto the back patio.

Stanley had disappeared. The police hadn't made it to the back yet. The coast was still clear.

Except that I didn't know where the secret passage was. There hadn't been one here this morning. And it wasn't like there were any signs or anything pointing the way.

No way I was hanging around, though. The police seemed to think I was some sort of criminal. I had to go somewhere safe and figure out what had happened.

The police were yelling in front of the house. I could hear more sirens coming. Then I heard an army of feet pounding around the far side of the yard.

I jumped up and dove over the bushes into Stanley's yard. Or at least, what I thought was Stanley's yard. I ran to the back, hopped the fence, and found myself on Cheshire Lane.

And right in the path of an oncoming mail truck.

There wasn't enough time to duck. I threw my hands in front of my face and prayed for a miracle. The next voice I heard was bound to be an angel's.

It wasn't.

"There you are, Mitchell! Quick, into the truck. Why do you have your eyes closed?"

Stanley was leaning out the passenger side of the truck. It had stopped an inch from my body. He grabbed me as the truck's driver, a short, balding man in a postal uniform, threw the vehicle into reverse. We plunged into the cab and slammed the door as the driver swerved down the road.

"What happened to you?" he asked as I struggled to get up on the seat.

"I couldn't find the secret passageway."

"What secret passageway?"

I realized that I was wet where I had fallen against Stanley. Then I saw that he was still drenched. His clothes were the ones he had been wearing when he fell into the kiddie pool.

"Why'd you change back into your wet clothes?" I asked. "And where's your tommy gun?"

"Roadblock!" shouted the postal worker before Stanley could answer. "Hide in the back, both of you!"

Stanley and I jumped into the back of the truck. The only place to hide was in the sacks of mail. So we opened a pair and slid in, covering our heads with envelopes.

The truck stopped and I could hear the mail carrier talking to one of the police officers.

"Nothing here but mail," he told him. "Neither rain nor snow nor roadblocks will keep me from delivering it."

I heard the back of the truck being opened. The vehicle rocked with the weight of someone climbing inside. Whoever it was started shuffling and kicking among the packages.

A boot caught me right in the ribs. I groaned into a bundle of flyers advertising the Reader's Digest sweepstakes.

I could hear some more shuffling. Then I heard the sound of one of the sacks being untied.

"Nothing here but a bunch of bills," complained a voice that must have belonged to one of the officers. "But we better look in all the sacks, just to be sure."

My sack was picked up. I could feel the top being loosened.

"Excuse me," said the mail carrier from the front. "But opening other people's mail is a federal offense."

"I wasn't opening the letters, just the sacks."

"Same thing," said the postal worker. "How would

you like it if someone opened your mail? What if they found out about your Uncle Lou?''

''Sorry,'' said the officer. He dropped me on the floor with a thud.

''What about your uncle?'' asked another cop outside.

''Never mind,'' said the officer, closing the back door.

''He got me right in the stomach,'' groaned Stanley when I opened his mail bag. ''Good thing I didn't have any lunch yet.''

''You didn't have pepperoni chili?''

''Yuck. Why would I have that?'' Stanley asked.

''You just told me you did. You were in my house.''

''No, I wasn't. The guy in the mail truck saw me and picked me up. He told me there was another me here, but I didn't believe it.'' Stanley was still bent over. ''Boy, I don't think I'll eat for a week.''

''So there *are* two Stanleys here,'' I said.

''And another Mitchell, too. Only they're nothing like you.'' The driver was nodding solemnly in the front of the truck. He pulled over to the side of the road, then turned toward us. ''You might say they're anti-you.''

''Anti-us?'' Stanley asked.

The postal worker nodded again. ''You'd better hope you don't run into them again,'' he added. ''Because if you do, you'll both be obliterated.''

"I don't know what *obliterated* means," said Stanley. "But I have a feeling it's worse than going to bed without any supper."

"Let me put it to you this way," the man continued. "If you touch the anti-Stanley, every atom in your body will cancel out every atom in his body. There'll be nothing left but a black hole where your body was. And then things will get *really* interesting. From an apocalyptic point of view, that is."

5

The mail carrier's explanation for what had happened to us sounded a bit like one of my dad's lectures on how a vacuum cleaner worked, only more confusing. If you stripped away all of the mumbo jumbo, it came down to this:

There are many possible universes. They all exist, all the time. They are all constructed of matter, or the exact opposite of matter. The opposite is called anti-matter. Anti-matter is kind of like the mirror image of matter—it's the same, only in reverse and backwards, like what you see in a mirror.

Stanley and I had stumbled into an alternative universe constructed of anti-matter. Things here were very similar to things in our Eerie. There were a few differences, like the fact that the statue was facing the wrong way. The most important difference, though, was the anti-matter. If the exact opposite particles touched each other, they would cancel each other out.

In other words, if the real Stanley met the anti-Stanley, there'd be nothing left.

"How do you know all this?" I asked the mail carrier when he finished.

"It's not rocket science," he said. "It's easy stuff. Every detail is on the exam you take to work for the post office. Where do you think mail goes when it gets lost?"

"To another universe?" Stanley asked.

The man nodded. "Otherwise, it'd be too easy to find," he said. "We trade our mail from universe to universe, moving it around until the price of postage goes up. Then it gets returned for postage due."

"Say, is my subscription renewal to *Action Superheroes Comix* in one of the bags back there?" Stanley asked. "Is that why the comic books stopped coming?"

The postal worker shrugged. I had to restrain Stanley from going into the back of the truck and sorting through the mail. We had more important problems than renewing comic book subscriptions.

The one question the worker couldn't answer was how we had managed to slip between universes.

"You weren't mailed, were you?" he asked.

"Nope," I told him.

"You didn't get stuck in a particle accelerator, did you?"

"What's that?" asked Stanley.

"It's like a very fast clothes washer on the spin cycle," said the man.

"I think they have one at the Eerie Laundromatic," said Stanley. "But we haven't been there in weeks."

That was the truth. The last time we were there— well, it's a very short story. And a tall one. I'll tell it to you sometime.

"My father has a particle accelerator at work," I said. "Believe me, we weren't anywhere near one. We were looking for the edge of strange with a homemade weirdness detector."

"Maybe your being here has something to do with the device you constructed," the mail carrier suggested. "Perhaps you managed to stand on a fissure."

"What's a fissure?" Stanley asked.

"Fissures are cracks or holes in the universe. They're fairly narrow—usually just big enough to slip an envelope or two through. If it's important, that is."

"So how did we fit?" I asked. "We're both bigger than envelopes."

The man shrugged. "It's hard to say. With the right sort of equipment, the hole can be made wider. You probably just got lucky."

"Or unlucky," I said, remembering the rock Stanley threw. "How do we get back?"

"Your best bet is to go back to the spot where you first noticed that things were different. Do everything you were doing up until that point—but in reverse."

"Can't we just go back with you?" Stanley asked.

"Oh, I won't be going back to your reality for a long time," said the postal worker. "I'm on the regular route—not priority."

Interesting—in the anti-Eerie, Stanley was me, and I was Stanley. And we were both our opposites.

Kind of makes your brain hurt just thinking about it, doesn't it?

Stanley's clothes were still wet. To dry them out, we turned on the defroster and had Stanley sit on the windshield for about ten minutes. It worked, but he came out a little wrinkled.

When he was dry, the mail carrier wished us luck.

"There's one more thing to remember," he said.

"What is it?" I asked. "That opposites attract? That if matter and anti-matter meet the universe will return to nothingness?"

"No. Always include the proper zip code on your mail," he said, closing the door to his truck and driving off.

*　　*　　*

The first order of business was to sneak back into the anti-Stanley's house and retrieve our homemade weirdness finder. Once we had it, Stanley and I could return to the edge of town, fiddle with the receiver, and with a little luck, land back in our own weird reality. Strange or not, I liked my own universe much better than where we were now.

There was only one problem. The police had the entire area sealed off. We couldn't get within a block of the house.

The cops weren't fooling around, either. They had their own tommy guns. Some patrolled on foot. Others sat on the fenders of their sleek old cars, just daring the bad guys—us—to show up.

"Maybe we can put on some disguises and sneak past," Stanley suggested.

"I don't think that will work. They're not letting anyone through."

"Maybe we could get one of the neighbors to help us."

"Too risky," I said. "We can't be sure what our neighbors are like in this universe. Some things are just a little different."

"Out of all the universes in the world, we had to pick one where we're bank robbers," complained Stanley. "Why couldn't we land in one where we're kings or something?"

"Wait a second. You—I mean, the anti-Stanley—told me that there was a secret passageway in the backyard. If we could find another entrance to it, we could use it to get back into the house."

"Sure, but where is it?"

A good question. There was no secret passageway in our reality.

Except . . .

The town historian, Mr. Neanderthal, told me that Eerie was once a stop on the underground railroad. Maybe that was the mirror universe's version of a secret passage.

"The tracks must have been torn up years ago," said Stanley when I told him. "And how's an old subway going to help us?"

"It wasn't a real railroad, Stanley. It was an escape route for slaves coming north before the Civil War."

"Oh, too bad," he said. "I thought you meant a real subway. We really could use one in Eerie."

"This was more of a collection of secret passageways and tunnels and hiding places," I explained. "Maybe it was the opposite of the secret passage here—since some things are a little bit off."

"Worth a shot," agreed Stanley.

"Mr. Neanderthal said the old Bailey place was a stop. That's less than a block from here."

We trotted over to the old house. Just like in our universe, it was three stories tall with peeling paint and a big sign on the front lawn that read KEEP OUT! NO ONE LIVES HERE, NOT EVEN GHOSTS.

We looked all around the yard, but couldn't find anything that looked like a secret passage. There were no caves, no disappearing doors, no signs that read SECRET PASSAGE, KEEP OUT.

Stanley suggested that we check the basement—a prime spot for secret tunnels. All the doors were locked, but a light was on and we could see through one of the basement windows easily enough.

It was empty. The floors and walls seemed to be made of solid concrete.

"There might be a secret passage down there somewhere," said Stanley. "Solid concrete would be the perfect disguise."

"I don't think so. I'm afraid we're going to have to come at this problem from a whole different direction."

"Maybe we could find someone with a particle accelerator and get propelled back into our universe," said Stanley.

Somehow, I knew that wouldn't be easy. Our best bet was still to sneak back and get our weirdness detector.

"Let's go see what the anti-World of Stuff is like," I suggested. I began walking toward the street, leading the way. "Maybe some anti-matter Black Cows will loosen up the gray cells in my brain and get me thinking again."

"What if they're not Black Cows in this universe?"

asked Stanley, trotting behind me. ''What if they're purrrrrr—''

I turned around and saw he wasn't pretending to be a cat. His words were echoing as he disappeared down a very deep hole just to the right of the path.

6

I pushed away the leaves covering the path. Then I threw myself on the ground and peered into the hole.

"Found the secret passageway!" Stanley shouted up. "Are you all right?"

"I have a bruise the size of Montana," he answered, "but otherwise I'm fine."

"Is there another way down?" I shouted. No use both of us getting hurt.

"Hold on, let me see," he replied. He stumbled around in the darkness, banged into a wall, then called back. "There doesn't seem to be a ladder here. Wait, here's a sign. Uh-oh," he said, reading. "Beware: Falling bodies ahead. Secret passage emergency entrance."

"Is that the only way down?" I asked.

He stumbled around some more. "Oh, wow, now I can see!" he exclaimed. "Funny how much clearer things are when you open your eyes."

"Quit fooling around, Stanley."

"Face the direction you were walking in, then take ten steps to your left," he told me. "See anything?"

A stone carving of a man with his forefinger in front of his mouth stood in the middle of the garden. He looked as if he were shushing the flowers. I walked over to the statue and gave it a push. Sure enough, it slid quickly out of the way, revealing a large ramp heading downward. A sign just inside read SECRET PASSAGE— HANDICAPPED ENTRANCE.

Stanley was waiting at the foot of the ramp. He shone a beam from a flashlight in my face.

"This is some setup down here," he said. "There are lockers in the walls with all sorts of supplies. Blue lights show you where they are. I got the flashlight over in that one there. And check this out—Air Supply."

He pointed to a button on the wall. I pushed it, and suddenly the tunnel filled with the sound of soft rock music.

"Boy, my mom would love this," Stanley said.

"Better turn it off," I told him. Air Supply was the name of an old rock band. "Someone might hear. Besides, I can only take so much geezer rock."

We began making our way in the direction where we thought our houses were. A dank odor filled my nose. The scent was a little hard to describe. Imagine your favorite gym socks, left out in the rain all night after a day of playing basketball. You go and put them in the wash, but forget to put any soap in. You start doing something before the wash ends, and forget about them for a week. They sit there the whole time, drying out on their own. Somehow they end up in your sock drawer.

The tunnel smelled like the drawer would when you found the socks.

Stones and bricks lined the walls. Every so often there was a box with supplies like the ones Stanley had found earlier. About twice the size of school lockers, the rectangular boxes were made of metal and built right into the wall. The writing on them read SECRET PASSAGE EMERGENCY SUPPLIES & OTHER COOL STUFF.

One thing I'll say for this anti-Eerie—they take their hidden tunnels very seriously.

Twice we came to forks. Both times we stayed to the right, figuring that was the right direction. Finally, the beam from Stanley's light caught a rusted iron rail against the wall. A ladder extended upwards.

"Must be the place," said Stanley.

"Must be." I put my hand on the nearest rung and pulled myself upwards. Stanley shone the light over my shoulder, but all I could see above was a dark hole and more ladder.

When I finally reached the top, I found a round steering wheel in the middle of the hole above my head. It was exactly like the sort of hatch door that submarines have. The wheel turned easily, as if it had been freshly oiled. Every so often I stopped turning and pushed upwards, hoping it would swing open. Finally, the latch slid free and the door moved upwards. But it was so heavy it didn't move very far.

Light flooded through the crack.

I was somewhere. In my backyard? Or across town?

And if it was my backyard, were the police nearby?

I gently closed the lid and pulled myself up another rung on the ladder.

"What's going on up there?" Stanley hissed.

"I have the hatch open," I whispered back. "Are you ready?"

"Go for it," said Stanley. "And don't worry—if you're caught, I'll escape."

"Gee, thanks."

"Don't mention it."

I held my breath. One hand gripped the wheel on the hatch door. The other gripped the ladder. Using my legs for leverage, I pushed upwards and threw the hatch door open. The bright light blinded me and I nearly lost my grip. For a second I teetered on the ladder, trying to regain my balance. I nearly slipped back into the hole.

Then I heard a familiar voice ask what I was doing.

It belonged to Mr. Crawford. The secret passageway led to World of Stuff.

To its frozen fruit section, to be exact.

"Hey, Mitchell, nice of you to drop in," he said, helping me up into the store. "Where's your friend Stanley?"

"Down in the tunnel."

"Well, come on up. I want your opinion on something."

The Mr. Crawford in this Eerie was a lot like the Mr. Crawford in our Eerie. He said that he'd just had a brainstorm, and decided to add pickled kumquats to his display. Stanley and I found ourselves staring at a huge pyramid of vinegar-soaked miniature oranges.

"Do you like the pyramid? Or should I make them into a cube?"

"I think the pyramid's just fine," I said. "We have to be going."

"Off to rob another bank?" he asked cheerfully, reaching both hands beneath his grocer's apron. "Not so fast."

Before I could say anything else, Mr. Crawford removed his hands from beneath his apron. In each fist he held a large pistol.

7

"The bullets in these guns have your names on them, boys," he said, pointing the weapons at us.

Stanley and I both put our hands up.

"W-what do you want?" I asked.

"Nothing. Consider them a loan," he said. Mr. Crawford held them out. He wasn't aiming them at us—he wanted us to have them.

Stanley reached to grab the one nearest to him. I held him back and told Mr. Crawford that we really didn't need them.

"But they're in good shape," he said. "Only used by a little old lady who robbed diners on Sundays. And not every diner, either. Just ones that didn't offer extra gravy with the meat loaf."

"Thanks all the same," I told him.

"They're in perfect shape. Here, watch."

Mr. Crawford fired one of the guns. The bullet whizzed down the aisle and hit a large cardboard display of the Jolly Green Giant. It glanced off his tooth and rebounded back, smacking one of the kumquats in the bottom of the pyramid. The fruit tumbled all over the place, covering half the store with a sheen of sweet and sour goo.

"Thanks, but no thanks," I told Mr. Crawford. "Come on, Stanley. We have to be going."

"I don't think I like this reality very much," Stanley said after we had shut the hatch tight and climbed back down into the passageway. "People seem to think being a criminal is cool."

"You're the one who thought Bonnie and Clyde were cool," I pointed out.

"That was different, Mitchell. That was a movie. It's not cool in real life."

I certainly couldn't argue with that. I also couldn't argue with the fact that if we didn't find a way out of this mess soon, we were going to be in big trouble. Even if we didn't meet up with our anti-matter selves, sooner or later someone was going to mistake us for them. Mr. Crawford already had. Anybody else might shoot first and ask questions later.

If they bothered asking questions at all.

"There's another ladder up ahead," said Stanley,

shining the flashlight along the tunnel. "Think we're at your house now?"

"Only one way to find out," I said, beginning to climb up.

I was twice as quiet opening the hatch this time.

Good thing, too. As soon as I cracked it open I saw the back of two black shoes and the pants legs of a police uniform right near the hatch. Quietly, I slipped the door back and climbed down.

"It definitely looked like my backyard," I told Stanley. "I could see some of the patio furniture. But there's a cop right next to the hatch."

"How are we going to get rid of the guard?"

"Maybe there's something in one of those emergency supply lockers we can use to distract him," I said. We walked back in the direction we came, looking for one of the lockers. Finally we found one. Stanley opened it and began rummaging through it.

"First aid kit, disguises, tax forms," he said, describing the items as he sorted through the locker. "Wait, here we go—distractions."

Stanley removed a large wooden box from the locker and placed it on the ground. Inside we found a deflated plastic doll. The instruction tag called it a "Pretend Damsel in Distress."

"It'll take too long to inflate," I said. "What else is in there?"

"Here's a can of fake fire," said Stanley. He read the instructions on the tag. "It works like a hand grenade. Just pull the pin, roll it on the ground and yell, 'Fire!' Hmm—it says this product is not to be used in a crowded theater."

The canister was just small enough to fit in my pocket. I climbed up the ladder again. When I reached the top, I hooked my right arm around a rung so I wouldn't fall. Then I began turning the wheel on the hatch. When I felt it click open, I stopped. I took a deep breath, getting ready. Pulling the pin out of the fake fire grenade, I pushed the hatch up.

Except that the hatch wouldn't budge.

I pushed again. Still nothing. The grenade in my hand began to make a sizzling sound.

I gave the hatch one more try. I had about as much of a chance of budging it as a beetle has of overturning a car. The cop must have gotten tired of standing where he had been—and was now standing on the hatch.

ZZzzzzz-zzz went the grenade.

Then it started to rattle.

"Look out below!" I yelled, dropping it. Stanley yelped, then dove against the wall as the grenade exploded with a burst of red light, and black smoke began filling the passageway. Desperate to escape, I slammed my arm against the hatch handle. This time, it flew upwards.

51

"Quick, Stanley! Up, up!" I shouted, leaping out of the hole.

Smoke and soot poured out with me. Coughing, I wiped my eyes clear. The officer who'd been guarding the backyard was standing right there. He'd heard the noise and stepped off the hatch, just in time for me to get out of the tunnel.

And just in time for him to capture me. I put up my hands to surrender.

"Devils! Devils!" he screamed, running in the opposite direction.

I spun around and saw Stanley emerge from the hole. Flames roared from the manhole behind him. I grabbed him and pulled him away, rolling him on the ground. I had to save him from burning to death.

"Mitch! Wait, wait!" he yelled. "I'm not on fire. It's fake, remember?"

He was right. Fake flames continued to shoot out of the hatchway. They looked exactly like real flames— red and orange and very, very scary—except that they weren't burning anything. In fact, they weren't even hot.

The smoke was real, though. It billowed up everywhere. The yard looked like the last time my dad barbecued.

"You look pretty gruesome," said Stanley. "You have grime on your face from the smoke."

"So do you," I said. "The cop must have seen the flames and thought we were devils."

"Lucky you're so ugly," said Stanley.

"Very funny. Let's go grab the weirdness detector and get out of here before he comes back with help."

We dashed to the back door of the house. The door was open and there didn't seem to be any other cops inside. There was a slight odor of tear gas in the air. Most of it had been sucked out by special tear gas vacuum cleaners, which were still running in the front hallway.

The last time I'd seen our homemade weirdness meter, the anti-Stanley had left it in the living room. But when I looked now, it was nowhere to be found.

"Maybe it fell behind a sofa cushion," said Stanley, pulling the pillows off the couch.

"It's too big." I threw myself to the floor and looked under all the furniture. No dice.

No weirdness finder either.

We quickly began running through the downstairs rooms, overturning tables, pulling things out, and looking in every possible hiding place. Stanley found a few coins and I found a comic book that looked suspiciously like the one I'd lost in my reality a few days before. But no weirdness detector.

Stanley ran upstairs to check the bedrooms. I finished looking through the magazine rack in the den, then went up to help. I had just reached the landing when I heard Stanley open a closet and say, "Wow—there's a shirt here just like I'm wearing!"

"No!" I shouted. "Don't touch it!"

But I was too late. Before I could take another step, a loud boom echoed through the hallway.

8

The explosion knocked me off my feet and back down to the landing.

I guess it wasn't the worst bang I'd ever heard. But it made me feel sick. Lying on the carpet, I dreaded getting up to see what had happened. I expected to see my friend in a zillion pieces.

Or no pieces at all.

I hadn't felt this sad since the school board voted to extend school an extra week. I got up and took two steps toward the room, not sure I wanted to see what I would see.

I was surprised to find Stanley lying in the middle of the floor. He wasn't wearing a shirt any more.

A shirt-shaped black hole hovered in front of the bureau.

"Wow, check it out," he said. "There's nothing there."

"The atoms in the two shirts must have canceled each other out," I said, examining the blank space. It was just like the postal worker had warned us. Matter had ceased to exist where the shirt and anti-shirt met. The space looked like the fuzz between channels on television. "There's now a size-eight hole in the universe."

"Size twelve," Stanley corrected me.

"Whatever. You're lucky you weren't sucked into it."

"Tell me about it," said Stanley. He nodded his head in amazement. "After I spotted the other shirt, I put it on the dresser. As I took off the one I was wearing, I felt it being pulled toward the bureau. Before I could let go, I felt a fuzzy feeling, a little like when a barber uses the electric hair clipper on your scalp. The next thing I knew, there was an explosion and I was lying on the floor."

"The shirts must have pulled themselves together," I told him. "You know what they say—opposites attract."

"I wonder what happens if you go into the black hole," said Stanley.

"Good question." I picked up a pair of socks from the drawer and threw them into the hole.

The socks disappeared without a trace.

Not all that unusual, I guess. Except that you usually only lose one at a time.

I threw a pillow from the bed into the hole. It was bigger than the hole, but it got sucked in anyway.

"Where do you think it went?" Stanley asked.

"I don't think we want to find out," I said.

"You're right," said Stanley. He went over to the night table and picked up the clock radio.

"What are you doing?"

"I've been trying to get rid of this dumb alarm clock for years," he said. "It's always waking me up."

I grabbed him before he could throw it into the hole.

"There's no telling what happens inside that hole," I said. "Besides—that's not your alarm clock. That's the anti-Stanley's. Yours is back in the real world. Come on. We still have to find my sister's TV and the rest of that stuff so we can get out of here."

Reluctantly, Stanley put down the clock. He went through the anti-Stanley's drawers and took out a fresh T-shirt.

"I wonder if this is *his* favorite, too," said Stanley. He pulled it over his head. "You know where I got this?"

"The Reading Railroad Museum?" I said.

"How'd you guess?"

"Maybe the words on the front gave it away."

We searched the rest of the house quickly. Both of us looked in all of our favorite hiding places back in the real world. But our homemade weirdness finder was nowhere to be found.

I knew the anti-Stanley didn't have it with him when he ran out of the house. But either he had come back for it, or the police had taken it when they searched the place.

Either way, it was time for us to leave—there were sirens outside.

I ran to the window and saw an old-fashioned black truck screech to a halt in the driveway. The words *Eerie Exorcism Department* were written on the side. A motto was written on the door: CALL US FOR ALL YOUR DEVIL-ISH SITUATIONS.

Four witch doctors got out, followed by an old lady with an incense burner. They began chanting and shaking large sticks with dozens of rubber balls tied to them.

Check that. They looked like rubber balls, but they weren't.

They were shrunken heads.

"I don't understand Latin too well," said Stanley. "But I think those guys are looking for us."

"They're not the only ones," I said as another truck drove up. A fresh troop of SWAT officers piled out the back.

We took the stairs three steps at a time, tumbling over each other as we tried to get out of the house. Already the exorcists were chanting at the front door. Just as we ran onto the back patio, another truck full of witch doctors screeched around the corner and slammed through the fence. Stanley and I dove for the hatch to the secret passage. We could hear chanting as we spun it closed.

I paused on the top rung, hanging there as I caught my breath. Once the doorway was locked, there was no way for anyone on top to get in.

Unless they had a key.

"Get the SWAT team back here," yelled one of the witch doctors above. "Have them bring the spare key for the secret passages!"

"Run for it!" I yelled to Stanley as I jumped off the ladder.

"Which way?"

"Any way," I said, following as he ran back in the direction we had come.

We went two or three hundred yards in the dark before we came to one of the emergency lockers. Stanley threw it open and quickly found a flashlight. In the distance, we could hear the sound of the hatch being opened.

Stanley started to go through the locker, looking for anything else that would help us. He took out a box that said THROW ON GROUND IF BEING FOLLOWED. Quickly, he threw it on the ground.

I heard a sound as if something had poured out, but

nothing else happened. It took a second before I realized millions of dirt-colored marbles covered the floor.

"Think it'll work?" Stanley asked.

"We'll have to hope so," I said, pulling my friend along as the first of the SWAT team's searchlights cut through the darkness of the tunnel.

We ducked left at the first fork. Behind us we heard shouts, screams, and splats.

"If we ever get back to our universe," said Stanley, "we should start working on a tunnel like this."

I didn't say anything. I couldn't decide which was more impossible: borrowing massive earth-moving equipment, or getting back to our world.

When we came to the next fork, we took a right. Then we came to an intersection with another passage. We kept running straight ahead. By now we were totally lost. But the SWAT team seemed to have stopped chasing us.

"Let's slow down a bit," Stanley said finally. We were both worn out from running, not to mention the rest of the day's adventures. Huffing and puffing, we walked a bit further and finally collapsed against the wall of the tunnel. I was more tired than dirt.

Assuming that dirt can be tired.

"Where do you think we are?" Stanley finally asked.

"Probably somewhere near the school," I guessed. I

took the flashlight from his hand. The beam showed that the tunnel continued straight for quite a way. As I moved the light around, I noticed that the passage here was slightly different from the part we had been in before. White tiles lined the ceiling. The walls were also covered in tile, but these tiles were various colors, arranged in artistic patterns.

"This place kind of reminds me of a subway I saw in a movie once," I told Stanley. "Except that there are no railroad tracks."

"Maybe they were torn up." He looked at the floor. "Or maybe they just poured dirt over them and packed it down."

"Let's get going," I said, rising. "We have to find our way out."

Stanley got up and started following me. We had walked only a short way when we came to another intersection. This time we turned right. As soon as we did, I tripped over something on the floor.

Stanley nearly did the same thing helping me up.

"What gives?" I said, struggling to my feet in the darkness. The flashlight had fallen a short distance away.

"Railroad tracks!" exclaimed Stanley.

He was right. The flashlight beam gleamed off the rail.

"Boy, you'd think it would be rusty after being out of use for so long," I said.

"Who says it's out of use?" said Stanley. "Look!"

I looked up and saw a dim yellow glow in the distance. As the tunnel began rumbling, I realized it was the light of a train, heading our way.

Right for us. On a collision course.

9

We started to run back the way we had come. After only a few steps, we realized we would never make it. The tunnel was now filled with the train's light.

"There's a ladder right there," I shouted to Stanley. "Quick!"

I bolted up the rungs so fast my head felt dizzy. The ladder ended on a flat piece of concrete. It looked like the platform at a station. I rolled out of the way as Stanley clambered up behind me. Meanwhile, the train's engineer must have seen us on the tracks. He slammed on the brakes and the train screeched to a stop right next to us.

Steam poured out of the engine. My nose stung with the odor of burnt coal and metal from the brakes. Rising to my feet, I saw that the engine pulled a train of five passenger cars. They looked old-fashioned, though even in the dim light from the train I could tell the paint was fresh. Lights were on inside the cars. They were filled with people. None of them bothered to look at us. They all seemed to be busy reading papers or talking or sleeping.

"Hey, you boys! Are you getting on or not?" someone shouted from one of the open doors. A conductor emerged from the car with a pocket watch in his hand. I realized we were standing in a train station. It looked like a subway stop, the kind you might find in a big city.

"Where are you going?" I asked the conductor.

"What do you mean, where are we going?" demanded the conductor, walking toward me. He gave me a suspicious look. "Were you kids playing on the tracks?"

"No."

His frown said he didn't believe me.

"Well, get on board if you're going," he said.

"Where's your next stop?" Stanley asked.

"Center of town."

"Do you go near the old mirror factory?" I asked.

"Of course," said the conductor. "Haven't you ever ridden the Eerie subway before?"

"No," I told him. "We, uh . . . we're new in town."

"Oh. Sorry," he apologized. "It's two stops away. Come on now. We haven't got all day."

"Um, what about our tickets?" Stanley asked.

"Tickets? Once you go through the turnstiles, you can go anywhere you want," said the conductor. "You did go through the turnstile, didn't you?"

"Yup," I said, shushing Stanley with a quick elbow. "It's just that we're new. Where we come from, you have to pay twice."

"Hmm, sounds like a good idea. Let's get a move on." The conductor began walking back to the train.

Stanley and I exchanged glances. If we got on the train, we could ride to the edge of town. We'd know where we were. But we'd also be trapped if the SWAT team somehow got on board.

Of course, we might get run over if we went any further on foot. The anti-Eerie was turning out to be very different from our Eerie. There was no telling what differences might prove fatal. This one almost had.

"We're coming," I told the conductor. I nudged Stanley and started toward the train.

"Hey, wait a second," said the conductor, putting out his hand. "You look familiar. Do I know you?"

"No, sir."

"You didn't rob this train a few weeks back, did you?"

"No way," I answered. He gave me another suspicious look, but then let me pass.

Stanley and I climbed into the old-fashioned car. It seemed to be made mostly of wood. Whoever polished it must have broken their elbows making it gleam. A thick red carpet lay on the floor. The passengers were all dressed in very fancy clothes. A few smiled at us as we walked down the aisle looking for seats. Most didn't look up from what they were doing.

The only seats open were halfway down the car. Stanley insisted on taking the window. We were barely seated when the train started to move.

"This is pretty nice," said Stanley. "We ought to get something like this in our Eerie." He wedged himself down. He looked like he was going to fall asleep.

"Don't get too comfortable," I told him. "We have to get off in two stops."

"Oh, you've got plenty of time, son," said the man in the seat in front of me. The seats were tall and I couldn't see him. "The next stop isn't for five hundred years."

"Very funny, mister," I told him. "The conductor just said—"

"Oh, I wouldn't listen to that conductor," said the man, rising. "He still thinks he's alive."

A skeleton head popped up over the back of the seat. As I screamed, I realized that everyone in the train was now looking at me—and they were all skeletons, too. A pair of bony hands grabbed me as I tried to rise from my seat. I tried to scream again, but ghoulish fingers clamped themselves over my mouth.

* * *

"Mitchell! Mitchell! SSSSHHHH! Wow, you could wake the dead!"

I opened my eyes and realized Stanley had his hand over my mouth. The tunnel was empty. It looked exactly as it had before—no tiles, no tracks, and most of all, no train.

It had all been a dream.

"Are you okay?" he asked.

"Yup," I gulped. "Now I am."

Sometimes dreams are messages from your brain. This one had told me that no matter how bad anti-reality was, it could be worse.

"While you were sleeping, I found a sign up ahead that tells where to go," said Stanley. "Come on. But be quiet. I think I heard something."

"Was it the SWAT team?" I asked as I got to my feet.

"No. You won't believe this, but it sounded a bit like a train." Stanley shook his head. "That's impossible, though. What were you dreaming about, anyway?"

"I'll tell you later," I said, quickening my pace.

The sign Stanley had found stood in the middle of an intersection not far away. It had names, distances, and arrows:

EDGE OF TOWN ¼ MILE→

↑¼ MILE UPTOWN EERIE

NEW JERSEY *WHY WOULD YOU WANT TO GO THERE*?

"I wonder why everybody dumps on New Jersey," I muttered, leading the way toward the edge of town. Even if we didn't have the weirdness detector, maybe we could find our way back from there. If the fissure the mail carrier had told us about really existed, then maybe we could slip back through.

After walking about fifteen minutes, we came to a ladder leading upwards. The hatch above looked like the one near the back of my house. There was no sign or anything saying where we were. I told Stanley to wait, then started upwards.

Something about climbing a ladder always makes me feel hopeful. It doesn't matter whether it's a little step stool or the big aluminum job my dad uses to clean our gutters. Climbing upwards makes me feel like I'm heading for an adventure.

Which isn't always a good thing.

Still, I couldn't help feeling good as I turned the wheel on the hatch. We might be totally stuck here with no way out, in danger of becoming black holes at any minute, but hey, no day is perfect.

As soon as I popped the hatch, I saw that this one was about to become even less perfect. The hatch sat in the middle of the sidewalk across from the abandoned mirror factory.

The anti-Stanley stood against the fence, staring directly at me.

10

"It's about time you showed up," said the anti-Stanley. "I've been waiting here for hours."

"Uh, sorry," I said.

"Well, are you coming out of the tunnel or what?"

I hesitated. The real Stanley was already starting up after me. If he came up, the anti-Stanley might figure out what was going on. Worse, the two Stanleys might come together and erase themselves.

No way I wanted a black hole for a best friend.

"Stanley," I said loudly, "you wouldn't believe what's happened to me. A SWAT team came and chased me through the tunnel."

"Big deal," said the anti-Stanley. He turned around and bent over something on the ground.

"I was there," mumbled the real Stanley from below. I had hoped my extra-loud voice would give him a hint that there was trouble. But it didn't.

Quickly I jumped out of the hole and slammed the hatch closed. I heard the real Stanley yelp below.

"What are you doing?" the anti-Stanley asked. His back was still turned away.

He was fiddling with my sister's television. It was sitting on the ground near the fence, along with the rest of the weirdness finder equipment.

"Just wanted to make sure the secret passageway is still secret," I said. I tried to act nonchalant, like nothing was going on. "A ton of SWAT people were after me."

"You should have turned on the anti-SWAT lights in the tunnel," he said.

"I forgot."

"You forgot? You were bragging about putting them in just the other day," said the anti-Stanley. "What's with you lately, Mitch? You're losing your edge. You used to be the best bank robber in the game."

"Getting old, I guess," I told him. I nodded at the TV. "What are you watching?"

"Up until a second ago, I was watching a rerun of *Leave It to Beaver*. Boy, I love that show—it is so unreal."

"Yeah. What happened?"

"I don't know. The reception went crazy. What's with this other junk you had attached?" he added, pointing to the homemade weirdness equipment. "I was going to throw it out."

I had to think fast. Except for the bank-robbing stuff, this Stanley had been a lot like my pal. He looked like him, talked like him, even yawned without covering his mouth like him.

"It's a little invention I've been working on," I said. "It will help me predict who's going to win the Super Bowl."

His eyes lit up—just like the real Stanley's would have.

"Really?"

I nodded solemnly. Stooping over, I picked up the equipment. It was all there, and seemed to be okay.

"I need two more things before I can get it to work," I said. "A football schedule and an autographed football jersey."

"I'll bet Old Man Crawford has both of those things down at World of Stuff!" exclaimed the anti-Stanley.

"Why don't you go and ask if we can borrow them?" I suggested.

"No way," he said. "Why should I walk all the way over there? It's your invention."

Like I said, the anti-Stanley and the real Stanley were very similar.

"You want to know who's going to win the Super Bowl, right?"

The anti-Stanley frowned. I could tell he wanted to. But he was also, well . . . lazy.

"I have to work out some more details for the bank robbery," I told him. "Go ahead. By the time you're back, I'll be finished."

"Oh, all right. I'll go," said the anti-Stanley. "But you owe me."

"I'll cut you in for a bigger share of the loot after the robbery," I said.

"You mean I'll get five percent?"

"Make it seven," I told him.

"Deal," he said happily. He trotted past me—then stopped at the hatch to the secret passage.

"Wait!" I shouted as he started to open it.

The anti-Stanley turned to me in surprise.

"The, uh, the SWAT team. They're still down there," I said. "They were all over the place."

"Oh, right." The anti-Stanley dropped the cover.

There was a groan from below.

"Did you hear that?" he asked.

"Yes, the television reception is clearing up," I said, pretending to fiddle with the set. "You better hurry if we're going to get this put together before the robbery."

"Yeah, you're right," said the anti-Stanley. "Say, Mitch—this time, can I shoot my name into the ceiling with the tommy gun if they don't hand over the money fast enough?"

"Sure," I told him.

*   *   *

"You dropped the hatch right on my head," said the real Stanley when I helped him out of the hole a minute later. "I can hear bells ringing. Sounds a little like an old Beatles song. 'She loves you, ga, ga, ga . . .' "

"Come together and help me get the weirdness detector working," I told him. "Before the anti-Stanley decides he forgot something and comes back."

"You think he will?"

"You would."

Stanley knew I had a point. He hurried over and helped me wire our contraption back together.

"You think this thing can really predict who will win the Super Bowl?" he asked. "I heard you tell the other me that."

"Oh, sure it can," I said. "And the World Series, too."

"Wow. Let's get it together fast."

Sometimes it's better not explaining a joke. We snapped the cables in place and tuned the television to channel 372, the all *Romper Room* station. But no matter how I turned the antenna, the screen was still filled with fuzz.

Stanley suggested we try walking up and down the street. We had taken two steps when we heard a muffled explosion back near the cover to the secret passage. The hatch flipped open. Men with rifles and gas masks emerged as smoke poured from the hole.

The SWAT team had finally tracked us down.

"Run!" I yelled, heading toward the mirror factory. The homemade weirdness detector nearly fell out of my hands.

"Yow!" yelped Stanley. A bullet whizzed by his head.

Then three more shot by.

The fourth seemed to disappear into thin air as we ran. I whirled around and grabbed Stanley's arm. We fell backwards, tumbling onto the sidewalk. The detector flew through the air, landing with a crash against the chain-link fence.

Somehow, the crash didn't hurt the TV. I glanced over and saw that the reception was as clear as ever.

Romper Room was on. We had returned to our own reality.

11

"Hey, is this the one where Mr. Bluejeans comes on?" asked Stanley, standing and pointing to the screen. "He comes in with some snacks for the kids, and then he tries to take them hostage."

"I don't think so."

"It is. Gee, this is great. I've never seen the ending."

"And you're not going to see it now," I said, switching off the television. "We've had about as much weirdness as I can stand for a day."

"Boy, going from one universe to another sure makes you grumpy," said Stanley. "Maybe you should drink more orange juice in the morning or something. Or try vitamins."

"I get plenty of vitamins."

"Man, you are touchy," said Stanley, stooping down to pick up a rock. "Here, come on. Let's see if there's any more glass left in the old mirror factory."

"Don't! This all started because you broke a mirror there," I told him.

"Oh, come on, Mitchell. Give it a rest." He whirled his arm back and let the rock fly. When it landed without breaking anything, he stooped down to pick up another.

Suddenly I felt very angry. I'm not really sure why. Maybe it was because I had just barely escaped from an anti-matter universe. Maybe I was worried about all the scratches on Kari's television. Or maybe I was mad because I'd never had a chance to eat that microwave pizza. Whatever it was, I started back toward home without waiting for Stanley.

I turned the corner and took about two dozen steps back toward the center of town. Then I realized how silly I was being. After all, Stanley was my best friend. We had just had an incredible adventure together. True, we hadn't found the edge of weirdness like we had set out to do. But stumbling into another universe and creating a T-shirt-shaped black hole isn't anything to sneeze at.

Besides, I knew Stanley's breaking the mirror had nothing to do with what had happened. That was just a coincidence.

Right?

Anyway, I couldn't stay mad at Stanley for very long. We were buddies. He'd saved me back in the anti-Eerie by finding the postal worker. Tomorrow I might have to save him. Who knew what kind of weirdness we would encounter? The important thing was, we would face it together.

As I turned back to apologize I heard a loud voice around the corner call to Stanley.

The weird thing was, it sounded just like me.

12

"*H*ey, Stanley, hold up. Why were you throwing rocks at the mirror factory?"

"What do you mean, why was I throwing rocks?"

"Don't you have anything better to do with your time?"

"Quit bugging me. How'd you get back behind me, anyway?"

I reached the corner and ducked behind a fence as they continued talking. Peering through the slats, I saw Stanley talking to someone a short distance away.

The person was me.

Or at least he looked exactly like me. Which could only mean one thing—the anti-Mitchell had somehow come across into our reality.

"Some SWAT guys chased me through the secret passage," he said. "I couldn't get rid of them for anything. And I kept hearing a train whistle everywhere I went."

"Are you okay?" Stanley asked the anti-me.

"Why?"

"You told me all this a little while ago. And I know about the SWAT guys because I was there."

"I told you this already?"

"How'd you change your clothes so fast?"

I knew that somehow I had to warn Stanley what was happening, but how? The anti-me was a big-time bad guy in his universe. He was probably ruthless. He might shoot Stanley, or worse.

On the other hand, if he and I touched each other, we'd be zapped into nothingness.

My dad says there's a solution to every problem. This one would have taken Einstein to figure out. But he was nowhere around.

"Why are you busting my chops?" demanded the anti-me. "Quit fooling around and let's get to work. Have you cased the bank yet?"

"What bank?" asked Stanley.

"Duh. The bank we're robbing in town. Trust a Lot and Save a Little."

"Oh, that bank," said Stanley. For a second, I thought he had finally caught on to what was happening.

No such luck.

"You've really lost your mind, Mitchell. Did you bonk your head in the tunnel?" he asked.

"You're the one who must have hit his head. Why are you acting so weird? Are you really Stanley?"

"Are you really Mitchell?"

They eyed each other suspiciously. I rose to my feet and yelled for Stanley to run away.

"Why?" asked a voice behind me.

Even before I turned around, I knew who I would find.

I led the anti-Stanley to the corner, where we met the real Stanley and the anti-me. After I introduced myself and warned everyone not to touch, I tried to explain the situation.

"Basically, there are matter universes and anti-matter universes," I said, repeating the mail carrier's explanation. "You're anti-matter."

"How do you know you're not the anti-matter?"

I had to agree I had a good point. I mean, anti-me did.

"We're opposite each other," I said. "That's all that's important. Whatever way you look at it, it's very important for us not to touch each other."

"Why?" asked the anti-Stanley.

"Because you'll turn into a black hole if you do," said the real Stanley. "Weren't you paying attention?"

"Who are you calling a black hole?" asked the anti-Stanley.

"You, Particle Brain."

"Don't call me Particle Brain, Atom Head."

If it weren't for the fact that they were wearing different clothes, I never would have been able to tell them apart. They were so similar that they used the same insults.

"You're the Atom Head," said the real Stanley. "You're not real, you know. I am."

"No you're not. I'm real."

"You don't even exist in this universe," said my friend.

"You don't think so? Touch me and find out."

"I just might."

I threw myself between them before they could try.

"Hard to imagine someone could be this stubborn in two universes," said the anti-me. "So your universe is the mirror image of ours?"

"Not exactly. The corn statue in downtown Eerie faces the other way."

"But otherwise, we're the same, just opposite?" asked the anti-me.

"Well, we're not bank robbers in our universe," said Stanley.

"Really? That's weird," said the anti-me. "You must be pretty boring."

"At least we're not criminals. Robbing banks is breaking the law," I told him. "It's a crime."

"Well, everyone does it where we come from," he

said. "It's like a game. Of course, not everyone's as good as we are. We're the best. We're sort of like heroes. Right, Stanley?"

The anti-Stanley nodded.

"Killing people makes you heroes?" I asked.

"Oh, we don't kill people," he said quickly. "We just take their money. We're the good guys. The cops are the bad guys."

I shook my head. I really couldn't understand how being bad was good, even in another universe.

If it weren't for the bank robbing, though, I would have to say the anti-Mitchell was a pretty nice guy. He seemed intelligent and was certainly good-looking.

It was kind of strange talking to him. I felt as if I were talking to a mirror.

"So if you don't rob banks," he asked, "what do you do?"

"Go to school," I said.

"Bor-r-r-ing," said the anti-Stanley.

"We do cool stuff, too," said the real Stanley. "Today we were trying to find the edge of weirdness."

"You did a good job of that," said the anti-me. "But how did we get here?"

"You must have been near us when I turned on the weirdness meter," I told him. "It widened the crack between the two universes, and you came through. I'm sure it will work in reverse. Just tune in to the *Romper*

Room channel and walk back up the block. You'll be back in your own reality in no time."

"Why?" asked the anti-me.

"Like I said, I don't really understand it all, and it will take too long to explain. Ask the guy who drives the mail truck when you get back."

"No, I mean, why should we go back? This place looks pretty comfy."

"You can't stay here," I told him. "You're the opposite of everything here. Your electrons go in the wrong direction."

"So? From what you told me, as long as we don't touch our exact opposites, we're fine."

"Yeah, but—"

"I don't think there are any buts," said the anti-me. "In fact, I think we ought to stay here for a long time."

"But you can't do that," I said.

"Sure we can," he told me. "If I understand what you said, no one will suspect we're bank robbers. We can rob a whole slew of banks without anyone suspecting us. Back in our universe, we're wanted by everyone from the National Guard to the dog catcher. Here, we're just a couple of innocent-looking kids."

"Yeah," said the anti-Stanley. "Sounds like fun."

"Why would you rob banks here?" the real Stanley asked.

The anti-me gave Stanley a puzzled look. "That's what we do."

"You'll get caught," I told him.

"Nah. We're too good." He laughed. "But the police might arrest *you* guys. Be kind of fun visiting ourselves in jail."

"I don't think it's very funny," I said.

"What kind of guns do you have here?" asked the anti-me.

"We're not helping you rob banks," I said.

He shrugged. "Suit yourself. Come along, Stanley."

"I'm not going with you," said Stanley.

"Not you. The real Stanley."

"I *am* the real Stanley."

"Shut up pip-squeak, before I punch you," said the anti-Stanley.

"I dare you."

"Knock it off," said the anti-Mitchell, grabbing his Stanley.

I grabbed mine, while the anti-Mitchell dragged his Stanley away. They jeered at each other for about two blocks. Both of them struggled to get loose, shouting things like "I'd like to show you what the big bang was made of," and "Just give me five minutes and I'll rearrange your molecules for you."

Proof, I guess, that in any universe, Stanley can be a major pain.

13

As soon as they were gone, I let go of Stanley. He fell forward and rolled on the sidewalk.

"Mitch, you wouldn't really let me touch him, would you?" he pleaded. "I only yelled that stuff because I thought you'd keep us separated. I don't want to spend the rest of my life as a black hole."

"Relax. They're not around anymore."

"Boy, that's a relief." Stanley got up and dusted himself off. "Man, that other Stanley is obnoxious."

I rolled my eyes.

"We're going to have to figure out a way to stop them," I said. "Otherwise, they're going to ruin our reputation. Or worse."

"Can't we just go to the police station and tell them what's going on?" asked Stanley.

"Would you believe it?"

Stanley thought about it a moment before shaking his

head. Then he added, "They didn't seem to have any guns. They won't be able to rob many banks without weapons, or at least an ATM card."

"My bet is they'll find guns soon enough," I told him.

"Where?"

"Where would we go if we needed something?"

"World of Stuff."

I nodded. "Come on, let's see if I'm right. We'll have to be careful, though," I added. "We'll have to go a way we wouldn't go, or they'll see us."

"That means, if we're going to go down Mockingbird Lane, we can't, but if we don't, we are?" Stanley scratched his head. "We may never get there."

"You're right," I said, picking up the weirdness finder. "Let's follow them instead."

The crowd that had come out for the soap opera audition was gone. World of Stuff was deserted, except for Mr. Crawford. He was putting his slow time to good use, rearranging the dust on the widget rack.

The anti-Mitchell and anti-Stanley walked in just like we would. Stanley and I had caught up a few blocks back, sneaking behind in the shadows. We watched through the store window as they took our seats at the lunch counter.

"Hey, boys, what can I do you for?" Mr. Crawford called over.

"How about a couple of machine guns?" asked the anti-Stanley. I saw the anti-Mitchell kick him under the counter. Watching them was, well . . . eerie.

"Don't think I know how to make that drink," said Mr. Crawford, wiping his hands as he walked over. "How about a nice round of Black Cows on the house instead?"

"Make mine with bourbon," said the anti-Mitchell.

"Me, too," said the anti-Stanley.

"Oh, ho, ho—you guys are such cutups. Makes me think about when I was young and fancy-free."

"Before the lobotomy?" asked the anti-Stanley.

"No, actually, after the third one," said Mr. Crawford cheerfully. "Before the electroshock, though. Didn't have a care in the world. Two Black Cows coming up," he laughed. "Black Cow with bourbon. Very funny. You boys should have your own TV show."

I could tell that our anti-matter selves had not been kidding about the bourbon, which is a kind of whiskey. I guess in their universe kids can drink alcohol. I'm not sure why you'd want to, especially in a Black Cow.

Mr. Crawford didn't know they were serious. He also didn't know that they weren't us. If he didn't do what they wanted, sooner or later there was going to be trouble.

I pulled Stanley away from the window. We snuck around the side of the building to the alley, then to the back door. Gingerly, I opened it and we crawled inside. I hoped Mr. Crawford might come for something in the storeroom. Then we could warn him.

We snuck past the spare cash register and the cupboard containing every nail and screw known to modern man. Crouching down behind the machine that ties shoes while you wait, we held our breath and listened.

The anti-us were still at the lunch counter. Their slurping echoed through the empty store.

"Yum," said the anti-me. "That was good."

His voice sounded like mine when I told my Aunt Louise the neon pink sweatshirt she got me for Christmas was the best present ever.

"So listen, Mr. Crawford, old buddy," continued the anti-Mitchell. "Do you have anything we could rob a bank with?"

"Rob a bank, Mitchell?" Mr. Crawford seemed confused. Part of me wanted Mr. Crawford not to help the bad us rob a bank. Another part didn't want him to get hurt. So I had mixed feelings when he shouted, "I have just the thing!"

I signaled to Stanley to keep quiet, hoping Mr. Crawford would come into the back. But instead, he went to the Wild West section of the store.

"Here we go," he announced, returning with a box

to the lunch counter. "The Jesse James Authentic Bank Robbing Kit. Six-shooters, misspelled hold-up note, and black vests and hats. Not bad, huh? Only slightly used," he added.

"I don't think it's for us," said the anti-me.

"I'll knock a buck off because of the bullet hole," he offered. "Look, it's in the back of the vest. No one will ever notice."

"We were looking for something a little more modern."

"Modern, yes," said Mr. Crawford. I could hear the wheels spinning in his brain from where I was. I guess he hadn't oiled them in a while. "I do have a computer program that will let you siphon money from any bank account in the world," he said finally. "Unfortunately, it's for a Macintosh, and I only have PCs here."

"Just a plain old gun will do," said the anti-Stanley.

"Gun, well. Hmm. There *is* the Bonnie and Clyde special. But you boys are a bit young for that," answered Mr. Crawford.

"Let us be the judge of that," said the anti-Mitchell. Mr. Crawford went off to another part of the store. The anti-us started talking between themselves at the counter. I couldn't hear them, so I decided to try crawling out into the back of the store. I signaled for Stanley to stay where he was, then slowly slipped inside. I made it to the Dead Animal department, where I hid in the muskrat display.

"Let's get rid of the old creep," I heard the anti-Stanley say.

"We may need him as a hostage later," whispered the anti-Mitchell.

"Who would want him back?"

"Good point."

Mr. Crawford returned with a violin case. His face was flushed with excitement. "Now, are you sure you boys are old enough for this?" he asked.

"Sure we are," said the anti-Stanley.

I was just wondering whether to jump out when I heard a commotion in the back. The next thing I knew, a short guy in a trench coat and old-fashioned hat walked out of the storeroom.

Stanley—pretending he was Humphrey Bogart.

If you've ever watched old gangster or detective movies, you've probably seen Humphrey Bogart. He was a movie star who played the greatest tough-guy detective of all time, Sam Spade. Nobody could beat Sam Spade. Or Bogart.

Stanley had his hand jammed inside his trench coat pocket. It looked a lot like a pistol. It was an old trick Stanley had learned from the movies.

"All right, youse." He sneered. "Let's go. Back away from the lunch counter."

Let me say this about Stanley—he's very brave and awfully loyal. He didn't want to see Mr. Crawford get hurt.

He also does a very poor imitation of Humphrey Bogart.

"What's going on here?" demanded the anti-Stanley.

"This is turning into a really exciting day," said Mr. Crawford, backing away from the counter. "First I sold out of chocolate licorice, now this."

"Get your hands up," said the real Stanley, motioning with his coat. "Mitchell, come out and frisk them."

Reluctantly, I rose. "I can't frisk the anti-me," I said. "Have Mr. Crawford do it."

"Wow, I'm seeing double," said Mr. Crawford. "I don't even remember going to a party last night."

"I don't think he has a gun under that coat," said the anti-Mitchell. He was two or three yards from Stanley.

"Think I'm bluffing, eh?" Stanley made a motion with his coat and the anti-Mitchell backed up. You never could tell with Stanley, no matter what universe you were in.

Then Stanley made a fatal mistake. He switched from doing a bad Bogart to a really lousy Clint Eastwood.

"Make my day!" he growled at the anti-Stanley.

In the next instant, the anti-Mitchell pounced. He grabbed Stanley's trench coat and spun him around. They wrestled for a few seconds. There was a shout and a quick thud as my buddy fell to the floor.

"I thought so," said the anti-Mitchell, wrestling a

drill from under Stanley's coat. He shook his head. "Black & Decker. Try a Craftsman next time." I took a step toward him. "Not so fast," he said. "If you come any closer I'll throw him into my Stanley. There'll be nothing left but a black hole. An improvement, maybe, but not one you want to make."

He knew me too well. I stopped in my tracks.

"Okay, Mitch," said the anti-me. "Where's that TV thing?"

"What TV thing?"

"Don't play dumb with me, or I'll drill a hole through your friend Crawford there."

"Make it in the head," suggested Mr. Crawford.

"Wait!" I shouted as the anti-Mitchell raised the drill. "I left it back in the alley."

"Go get it, Stanley. Not you," he added to the real Stanley, who was struggling in his grip. He pulled up hard on the jacket, choking him. "The *real* Stanley."

"I *am* the real Stanley," said my friend, coughing.

"Hey, were you really going to throw that runt into me?" protested the anti-Stanley.

"Just get that TV thing." The anti-me shook his head and looked at me. "Maybe we ought to trade them for a while." Stanley tried to squirm away, but he tightened his grip. "Cut it out or I'll lock you in the back room and make you watch reruns of *F Troop*."

"One of the best television shows ever made," said Mr. Crawford.

"Get your hands up," the anti-Mitchell barked at him.

"Sorry."

"You can't stay in our reality," I told the anti-me. "Sooner or later, you'll be caught. Or worse—you'll turn into a black hole."

"If I go, you go," he warned. "Just remember that."

The anti-Stanley returned with our weirdness finder. "All the television channels are messed up here," he said. "I can't find the Candy Shopping Network."

"Channel seventy-five," said the real Stanley.

"All right, here's the plan," said the anti-Mitchell. "We'll take the tommy gun out of the fiddle case there, then we're going to rob the bank. You, Mitchell—you're going to find us a getaway car and wait by the bank."

"But I can't drive!"

"Why not?"

"Kids don't drive in this universe. Not until they're at least sixteen."

"Boy, you guys really live in a boring place, you know that?" said the anti-me. "No bank robbing, no car driving—back where I come from, you'd be just a couple of bad apples." He shook his head. "You better find a way to have a getaway car waiting in front of the bank in an hour, or your friend is history in *every* universe. Just get the car there,'' he added as I started to protest. ''I'll drive it away.''

The anti-Stanley opened the violin case that contained the Bonnie and Clyde special.

Then he held up an antique violin.

''What's this?'' the anti-Stanley demanded.

''A violin,'' said Mr. Crawford. ''Were you expecting a fiddle?''

14

I wracked my brain the second I left World of Stuff. Somehow, I had to figure out a way to stop the anti-us from robbing the Eerie Bank. But how? And how could I free Stanley and Mr. Crawford?

There was exactly one hour to think of something. As I headed toward my house, I caught sight of a postal truck. If postal employees went into different universes to lose mail, they probably ran into themselves all the time. A postal worker was bound to know how to deal with the problem.

But the truck turned a corner and disappeared before I could catch up. Since it was now Saturday afternoon, the post office itself was closed. The best I could do was the Fed Ex counter at the movie theater snack bar.

"Sorry, kid. We try not to lose anything," said the clerk at the counter. "And I can't seem to find the schedule for shipping to Other Realities. Come by on

Monday and ask for Flo. If anybody can get you into an alternative universe, she can.''

I was so dejected I was tempted to give up. In fact, I almost checked out the movie *Snow White and the Seven Dwarfs meet King Kong*. It had gotten good reviews, after all. And the posters were pretty cool.

But I knew if I did that my buddy Stanley would be toast. So I pulled myself together and began trotting home. My father was a scientist; he might have a solution.

If not, maybe I could talk him into driving the getaway car.

I had just passed Mrs. Smith's yard at the corner when her laundry gave me an idea.

When we were in the other universe, Stanley had taken a shirt from the anti-Stanley's drawer. If I could find the counterpart of that shirt here, I might be able to create a black hole. Then maybe I could trick the anti-us into going into it. We'd be rid of them.

But I had to be quick—the bad us would rob the Eerie Trust in less than twenty minutes.

My first stop was Stanley's house. No one was home. That was partly bad—it meant that I had to break in, because all the doors were locked. But it was partly good—I wouldn't have to explain to anyone what I was doing. Plus, I wouldn't have to find an excuse not to eat any of Stanley's mom's pie. She was always stuffing me with something when I came over. Between you and me, she cooks the way Attila the Hun sewed.

I'd never had to break into Stanley's house before. Getting past the storm window to the den in the back wasn't that difficult, though.

Getting past the electrified window gate was another story. As soon as I touched it, I felt myself being propelled back to the ground. My whole body twitched and trembled. If I had been holding a glass of milk in my hand, I would have turned it into a milk shake.

It also would have spilled all over the place.

But this was no time to be making milk shakes. I got up and looked for another way in.

Stanley's bedroom window on the second story was open. That was perfect. It didn't have a shock gate. But how to get up there? The ladder was in the garage. I decided to try shimmying up the drain pipe.

Not a horrible idea, except that it wasn't nailed to the house very well.

I got about three quarters of the way up when it started to pull away. At the first sound of creaking nails, I pushed myself upward. Somehow, I managed to catch hold of the roof gutter as the drain pipe fell to the ground.

Whoever had nailed in the drain pipe had also put the gutter together. It started pulling away, too. Closing my eyes, I swung my legs up onto the roof. Grabbing a shingle, I hung on as the gutter crashed to the ground with a crunch.

The open window was only a few feet away. The distance felt as if it were ten miles as I dragged myself across the roof toward it. Finally there, I dove through the opening and landed in a pile of Stanley's dirty socks.

Talk about torture. If the army ever runs out of bombs, they can just jam a few of Stanley's socks into their cannons and fire those instead of cannonballs. The enemy will surrender in no time.

Holding my nose, I ran to his drawers and started looking for the shirt.

I guess everybody has a different system for organizing their clothes. Most people probably put the shirts with the shirts, the pants with the pants. Or maybe they have a good clothes drawer and a bad clothes drawer. And I guess a few people arrange things by color.

But not Stanley. Stanley arranged his clothes according to alphabetical order. And not like ''S is for shirt,'' either.

Each item had its own special name. Like ''what I got for my birthday from Uncle Jim'' or ''dumb pants that I always trip over'' or ''kinda purple sweat socks.'' It probably made a lot of sense to Stanley. To anyone else, it looked like a big mess. I emptied all of the drawers, but didn't find the shirt.

Time was running out. Where could the shirt be?

I ran to the hamper in the laundry room. Luckily, I found it about halfway down, beneath some wadded-up towels.

Unluckily, it had the world's biggest tomato sauce stain in the middle of it.

Maybe not the world's biggest. But it would have been in the running. There was no time to clean it. The best I could do was squirt some stain remover on it. Then I ran it under the faucet. Most of the stain was still there.

There wasn't time to do any better. I hoped this wouldn't ruin the black hole.

I took a folded sheet from the closet. Then I ran to the garage, grabbed a crowbar and Stanley's bike, and set off for the bank.

15

About the last thing I expected to see in front of the Eerie Trust was the real Stanley with a machine gun.

"About time you got here, Mitchell," he growled. He was wearing a scarf over his face. "We're already robbing the bank."

"What do you mean, 'we'?"

"Yeah. I promised the guys you'd be here in time. What are you doing with the sheet and the crowbar? Where's the getaway car?"

"There is no getaway car," I said. "What's with the scarf?"

"All bank robbers wear them."

"Take off your shirt," I told him.

"No way. Take off your own shirt."

"Come on, hurry up before they come out of the bank."

"What are you doing?" asked Stanley. He lowered the scarf so he could talk better. "Mitchell isn't going to like this."

"I'm Mitchell."

"I mean the other Mitchell."

"He's a bank robber. And he's from another universe!" I shouted. "We have to stop him before he goes on a crime spree."

"He's not that bad a guy once you get to know him. The other me's not that bad either." Stanley pointed his gun at me. "You know, Mitch, living a life of crime might be fun."

"Stanley, if you don't take off that shirt, I'm going to pull this one over your head," I said, holding up our universe's version of the shirt. "You'll wear a black hole with a sauce stain for the rest of your life."

"But I love this shirt. I got it at the Reading Railroad Museum."

"Take it off!"

"You could at least have washed it," he said, reluctantly removing the T-shirt.

There were screams inside the bank. The robbery sounded like it was in full swing. I took the crowbar and pried off the manhole cover directly in front of the bank entrance. It weighed a ton.

My plan was to create the black hole down a foot or so in the sewer. Then I would cover it with the sheet.

When the two bad guys came out, they would fall through the manhole and be swallowed up. Once I replaced the cover, no one in Eerie would be in danger of falling into the black hole.

But when I took off the cover and held the stained shirt over the hole, I saw that my plan wouldn't work. The stained T-shirt wouldn't quite stretch from one side to the other. There was no way to keep it in place. And I could feel it being pulled toward Stanley's shirt, which he was holding in his hands.

I could just lay them on the sidewalk. But that would mean that there would be a black hole in downtown Eerie.

Maybe no one will notice, I thought as I crouched over the shirt.

Suddenly there was a shout behind me. The doors flew open and the anti-us came running out of the bank. They were wearing scarves just like Stanley's. There was a gun in the anti-Stanley's hands.

A very large, nasty-looking pistol. The kind that can ruin your day, and every day after that.

"Where's the getaway car?" barked the anti-Mitchell. His scarf fell down off his chin as he talked. There were two sacks of money in his hands.

I stood up and folded my arms. "There is no getaway car. I'm not helping you."

"You will or I'll fill you full of lead," said the anti-Stanley.

"Hey, leave my pal alone," said the real Stanley. I was glad that he had come back to my side, until he added, "He may be a jerk, but he's still my friend."

Gee, thanks, I thought.

"Hey, nice chest," the anti-Stanley told the real one.

"Thanks."

"Quick, down the manhole," barked the anti-me. "We can get to the secret passage and escape."

"There are no secret passages in this universe," I told him. "Guess you're out of luck."

"That does it," said the anti-Stanley, pointing the gun at me. I threw my hands out and closed my eyes as he pressed the trigger.

He got me right in the face.

With water.

Mr. Crawford had given them a realistic water gun. I should have known he wouldn't give them anything truly dangerous.

It took a second for me to realize that I was still alive. Stanley's T-shirt lay on the ground between us, and he was still clutching the anti–T-shirt.

Now or never, I thought.

"Stanley, throw that shirt down," I yelled. "Throw it on top of this one. Throw it!"

Stanley hesitated, then tossed the anti-shirt toward its mate. The two leaped together. There was a loud popping noise, followed by a jaw-snapping explosion. Then a shirt-sized blackness appeared in the middle of the sidewalk.

It looked just like the hole that had been created in the anti-Stanley's room. Except for the spaghetti stain.

"What's this?" said the anti-Stanley, peering down. "Is there a train in there? Do I hear a train?"

In any universe, Stanley is too curious for his own good. One second, the anti-Stanley was leaning over the sidewalk, peering into the blackness. The next second, he had vanished inside it.

"Hey! What did you do with my buddy?" demanded the anti-Mitchell.

"I'm not really sure," I admitted. "I think I sent him back to your universe."

I fudged because I hoped he would think it was safe to go into the hole.

No dice. The anti-me was as smart as the real one.

He pointed at the hole. "He went in there. Where does it go?"

"It doesn't go anywhere," Stanley blurted out. "It's the black hole that's created when matter and anti-matter meet. Just like we told you."

"Get out. I hear a train down there," said the anti-me. He peered into it. Suddenly, the bank alarm started to ring. I could hear a police siren in the distance.

"All right, we've fooled around long enough," said

the anti-Mitchell. He stood up straight. "You, into the hole," he told Stanley.

"No way."

"In there. Or I'll grab your friend and black him out."

"Like I care," said Stanley.

"You're as bad as the real Stanley!" shouted the anti-Mitchell. "You're going in first!"

As he reached for my friend, I grabbed the sheet from the ground. It spread as I whipped it over the anti-me. With the material between us, I could grab him safely.

At least I hoped I could.

Lunging toward him, a single thought popped into my head:

If this doesn't work and I vanish into nothingness, I'm going to feel awfully empty.

16

The bags of money dropped to the sidewalk. The sheet fluttered around and between us. We wrestled, matter versus anti-matter.

"Let go of me! I'll get you! I'll turn you into a blank space!" shouted the anti-me.

We rolled together on the sidewalk, arms flailing. Since we were exactly the same, the fight was exactly even. He rolled and got on top of me. I rolled and got on top of him. He knew what I would do. I knew what he would do. It was as if I was fighting myself.

As a matter of fact, I *was* fighting myself.

Weird.

Every so often, the sheet slipped a little. I felt myself being pulled toward the anti-me. It took all my strength to keep from touching him. If we had been wearing the same clothes, we would have been blanked out in no time.

Finally, he managed to elbow me in the gut. As I curled away, he leaped to his feet. The sheet fell away.

"Into the hole!" he shouted. He grabbed the sheet. Then he bent over to push me.

That's when Stanley gave the anti-me the best downfield block I've ever seen.

The anti-Mitchell flew threw the air. He landed in the black hole—and was sucked into oblivion.

I grabbed Stanley before he was sucked in, too.

It took a second for us to catch our breath. Slowly, we got to our feet. The black hole with the spaghetti stain lay on the sidewalk. The anti-us were somewhere inside.

"It's funny, but I hear a train, too," said Stanley, peering at the hole.

I grabbed him.

"I'm not sure about what happens in there," I said. "But I think you'd better not go very close. You saw what happened to the other you."

A police car pulled up and two officers jumped out. One of them spotted the money and scooped it up. Then they ran into the bank.

"Get rid of the water pistol and the scarf," I told Stanley. "Quick!"

"Where?"

"Into the black hole."

"Not so fast!" said a postal worker, appearing out

of nowhere. He grabbed Stanley. "Are those items properly addressed?"

"Uh . . . no," said my buddy.

"And no stamps, either," said the man, examining them. He shook his head. "Don't you know that something can't be lost in the mail if it's not properly addressed and paid for?" He leaned down and looked at the shirt-shaped hole we had punched in the universe.

"Watch out!" I shouted. "It's a black hole!"

"Without a zip code, I might add," said the postal worker, straightening up. "Although the spaghetti stain is a nice touch."

He reached into his leather case and pulled out a large manila envelope. Somehow, he managed to get the black hole into the envelope. "I'll just take this back to the central office, if you don't mind," he said. "We can't have black holes opening up just anywhere. One of our competitors might decide to go into the mail-losing business. Then what would happen? I'd be out of work."

EPILOGUE

*S*tanley and I didn't hang around very long after that. Even though the bad guys had been wearing scarves when they robbed the bank, we worried that the police would think we were them.

They might have, too, except that when they checked the surveillance camera there were blank spaces where the robbers should have been. It looked like two scarves and a water gun robbed the bank. I guess anti-matter doesn't photograph very well.

Since the money had been recovered, the police put it in a file of mysterious happenings and let it go at that. My guess is that file has gotten pretty thick lately.

The bad guys had left Mr. Crawford tied up in World of Stuff's Rope and Knots section. When we freed him, he acted like this sort of thing happened every day.

"Reminds me of the year I spent with a split personality," he told us late that afternoon. "Got so I was always going in the opposite direction of where I had been before I got there.''

Stanley and I exchanged glances. Normally when Mr. Crawford says stuff like that we don't understand what he means. But we did now.

The anti-us had left my sister's TV set and the rest of the homemade weirdness detector stuff in the store. The television was pretty banged up by now. Luckily, Mr. Crawford had some bang and bruise remover. He had the set looking like new in no time.

I decided we'd put off finding the other end of weirdness for a while. There's only so much strangeness anyone can deal with in one week.

''Say, did you boys hear what happened with the soap opera audition?'' asked Mr. Crawford, sitting down at the counter with us.

''No,'' I said.

''Turned out they only want one person from town.''

''Was it my sister, Kari?'' I asked. She's the world's biggest soap fan, so it wasn't a wild guess.

''No, it was me,'' said Mr. Crawford. ''Said I had the Eerie look.''

''Wow. When do you start filming?'' asked Stanley.

''Oh, I didn't take it. Who would mind the store? Besides, me on television? I don't think I could stand looking at myself.''

''I know what you mean,'' I said.

"And all that excitement? Too much for me. I like things the way they are," he added. "Boring."

Stanley and I rolled our eyes.

"I guess really being Bonnie and Clyde wouldn't be that cool," said Stanley as he slurped up the last of his Black Cow. "Being bad is just bad."

"You're starting to sound like Mr. Crawford," I told him.

"No, you know what I mean. Robbing banks, shooting at people—it's not what it's cracked up to be."

"You can say that again."

"I was kind of sorry to see me go," he added. "The other me, I mean."

"Why? He was obnoxious, overbearing, and stubborn," I pointed out.

"Yeah," said Stanley. "On the other hand, he did have a few bad points, too."

"Don't we all," I said, finishing my drink.

*N*o one looks forward to Christmas more than I do. Cool presents under the trees, dazzling lights on the streets, strange people singing off-key at your door. . . .

Well, okay, I can do without the bad singing. But the other stuff is "way wow," as my sister, Kari, likes to say. I love wrapping presents, and opening them, too. I love checking out the different window displays, and watching people nearly fall off ladders putting up lights on the edges of their roofs. Sitting by a Christmas tree with a hot cup of cocoa watching a train blow smoke rings through the tinsel really warms my toes. I even like my Aunt Louise's fruitcake. No one else in the family can say that with a straight face.

So I don't know what got into me this past Christmas. Maybe it was because of all the weird stuff that's been happening around town lately. Or maybe it was because even the best of us can lose sight of what's truly important.

It all began exactly two days before Christmas—or the eve of Christmas Eve. It was a Tuesday morning, the last day of school before our big Christmas and New Year's vacation.

For once, I was actually looking forward to school that morning. The last day before a long holiday was always easy going. I knew there would be no quizzes, no tests, no surprise homeroom shoelace inspections.

Yup, shoelace inspections. They started right after things got weird in Eerie. The teachers check your shoelaces to make sure they match. If they don't, you have to write a composition on why shoelaces are the second most important invention of all time, right after tissue paper.

I told you this town is strange!

But this being two days before Christmas, I knew I wouldn't have to worry about any of that. All I had to do was show up and go to an assembly on the many meanings of Christmas. I'd sing a Christmas carol, watch a skit or two, and then it'd be "so long and see you later" for a whole two weeks. My buddy Stanley and I had already drawn up a list of things to do with our free time, starting with ten haunted houses we wanted to inspect.

I was so excited I was the first one up in my house that morning. I went downstairs and poured myself a bowl of breakfast cereal—Popped Chocolate Sugar Surprise Flakes with extra sugar and frosted raisins. The box had a great motto: SWEET DAYS START WITH SWEET MEALS.

I like my flakes soggy, so I turned on the radio while I waited for the milk to soak in. The local station was playing music in between traffic reports.

Since there's hardly any traffic in Eerie, even at rush hour, that made for a lot of music.

"Here's a little number by our own local singing group," announced the DJ. "They call themselves the Three Wise Guys. They're the hottest thing to hit town since toaster tarts."

The song began. It sounded a lot like "Frosty the Snowman," except for the words:

> *Horace the snowman*
> *Was an Eerie kind of guy*
> *He was made of snow*
> *And had a purple glow*
> *Just the same as you and I. . . .*

"Boy, I just love this time of year," said my dad, walking into the kitchen. "Christmas carols, nonalcoholic eggnog for breakfast—it doesn't get much better than this."

He went to the refrigerator and took out the pitcher of eggnog mom had made the night before. The music on the radio changed to another old Christmas song, "Santa Claus is Coming to Town."

"My favorite Christmas song!" said Dad. "Mitch, do you know what this song is really all about?"

"Well . . ." I swallowed a big spoonful of my cereal.

"I know what you're thinking—it's about Santa Claus bribing little kids to be good by bringing them tons of spiffy new presents. But that's not it. Not at all," said Dad.

My father's a physicist at Eerie University. He likes to use everyday stuff to explain complicated physical phenomena. Like how the back fin on a '56 Chevy demonstrates how a comet works.

According to him, "Santa Claus is Coming to Town" proves Einstein's equation $E = mc^2$.

He said it has to do with the Uncertainty Principle, and being naughty or nice. Even though he'd explained it to me every Christmas I'd been alive, I still had no idea what he meant.

About halfway through his explanation, I asked for more orange juice. Throws him off the track every time.

By the way, my favorite Christmas carol is "Grandma Got Run Over by a Reindeer." Dad says that one proves Newton's laws of motion, but I just think it's funny.

"I'm glad you're up so early, Mitch," my father said, setting down my orange juice. "I need a little advice."

"From me?"

"That's right. I want to buy your mother a special Christmas present," he whispered. "Did you know her watchband is broken?"

"Do I! She complained about it all last week."

"Well, take a look at this," he said, unfolding a piece of paper. It was an advertisement he had cut out from the *Eerie Times*. "It's the Rolls Royce of watchbands."

Called the King Midas watchband, the thick strap was made of solid gold, guaranteed always to shine. Not only that, but it contained a special attachment that told you what the temperature was, and another that flashed excuses for being late, like "A 747 landed on the highway in front of me while I was driving here."

"Mom will love it," I told him.

Dad smiled. "Glad you like it. I'll pick it up this afternoon, right before the Eerie Christmas pageant. Don't tell her, okay?"

"Mum's the word," I said, sealing my lips with my cereal spoon.

"I really outdid myself this Christmas," said my father. "Heck, I think I even outdid Horace Feedlestake."

"Who's he?" I asked.

"He was the champion gift-giver when I was in sixth grade," explained my dad. "He found a way to package an entire snowstorm and present it to some kids who lived in the desert so they could have a white Christmas."

"Wow, they must have loved that," I said.

"Not really. No one had ever seen snow in the desert before. There were a lot of traffic accidents and the town had to close down for a week. It was a great idea, though."

"What was a great idea?" asked my mom, entering the room.

"Eggnog," said my dad quickly. "Who would have thought that putting eggs and nog together would make something that tastes so good?"

Mom gave him a funny look. I think she was about to explain that there is no nog in eggnog, but just then the phone rang.

"I'll bet that's for me," said my dad. "I'll take it in the other room. It's probably my boss telling me I can take the day off."

My mother waited until Dad was out of the room. Then she bent down and whispered to me.

"I'm glad you're up so early, Mitch," she said. "I have a question for you."

"I don't think there's any nog in eggnog."

"No. I want to buy your father a special Christmas present," she said. "You know how battered his old tool case is. Do you think he would like a new one?"

"Would he! He's always complaining that he's going to lose a screwdriver or bend his saw."

"I was hoping you'd say that." Mom took out an

advertisement she had clipped from the *Eerie Tattler*. "What do you think of this?"

It was an ad for the Toolcase 2000. This was a very serious tool case. Not only did it hold tools, but it dispensed advice on how to do any fix-up job known to humans. It also came with a handy list of excuses you could use to take the day off.

Pretty much the Rolls Royce of tool cases, as my father would say.

"It's a great gift," I told her. "That'll knock Dad out."

Mom smiled. "Glad you like it. I'll pick it up this afternoon, right before the Eerie Christmas pageant. Don't tell him, okay?"

"No way," I said, smiling back.

She took out her laptop to check her E-mail while she made some eggs for herself. I started humming a little song to myself. I couldn't help myself—if Mom and Dad were getting these great gifts for each other, just imagine what I would end up with.

"You're really outdoing yourself this Christmas," I told my mom. "You're even going to top Horace Feedlestake."

"Your father's old friend from school? Oh, he's not that hard to outdo. Imagine, sending snow to Eskimos."

"I thought it was to people in the desert."

"No, he sent sand to the people in the desert."

I was in such a good mood that I didn't even bother to try sorting out which of my parents was confused. I took another blissful, sugary bite of cereal and told myself this was going to be the best Christmas yet.

Then my dad came into the room with a frown that could have sunk a ship.

"This is the worst news I've ever had!" he said. "Christmas in the Taylor household is canceled! I've just been fired!"

THINGS CAN'T GET ANY EERIER
... OR CAN THEY?

Don't miss a single book!